Derek
Vivian Ward

ONLY ME

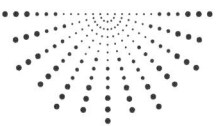

VIVIAN WARD
DEREK MASTERS

ALWAYS BOOKED PUBLISHING

Copyright © 2017 by Derek Masters

All rights reserved.

No part of this book may be reproduced in any form or by any electronic or mechanical means, including information storage and retrieval systems, without written permission from the author, except for the use of brief quotations in a book review.

For my Family

DEREK'S DARK DESIRES

Subscribe to my Dark Desires newsletter and get a FREE copy of Riot instantly! Riot is a full-length novel that is only available to subscribers!

Once you have your free book, you will have the advantage of knowing when I will be releasing my next title, when I'm having special deals, and you'll be the first to know the next time I have some cool stuff to give away (you can unsubscribe at any time).

newsletter.derekmasters.com

VIVIAN WARD NEWSLETTER

Get free books, ARC opportunities, giveaways, and special offers when you sign up for Vivian's newsletter. We all get enough spam so your information will never be shared, sold or redistributed in any way. You'll instantly receive a free novel just for signing up that isn't available anywhere else!

newsletter.authorvivianward.com

CHAPTER ONE

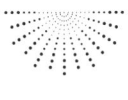

LUCAS

The sun is streaming through the curtains, threatening to scorch my corneas even though my heavy lids are closed tightly. I've been nursing my hangover all day, but it hasn't let up despite being almost 5 in the evening. Hopefully, when the sun goes down, it won't be as bad.

Today's no different than any other day though. Every morning I wake up, and she's the first thing on my mind. Her name is inscribed in my brain: Toni. She's usually the last thing I think about before I go to sleep and the first thing that pops in my head every morning.

Leaning over the edge of my bed, I reach for the bottle of ibuprofen that has a permanent home on my nightstand because of days like today. I guess I can thank the St. Louis City police department for not having to work today since they were the ones who had my driver's license suspended for DUIs; not that it's stopped me from driving, but I've had to limit the jobs I can accept.

Instead of taking bids for construction jobs in Illinois, all over Missouri, and parts of Kansas, I'm limited to what's right here in the immediate St. Louis Metro area. Thank God for rebuilding downtown or I might've been homeless, but right now, I'm appreciating the break while it lasts.

As soon as I successfully complete these mandatory AA meetings that the judge recommended, I can get my license back and won't have to worry about losing my construction company.

I guess there's no one to blame but myself, but blaming yourself sucks, so I blame it on life and the legal system. As high as the crime rate is on the North Side, you'd think the cops would have better things to do than pull someone over because they forgot to use a turn signal. There are about a billion theft crimes, sexual assaults, arsons, and drug traffickers to keep them busy until the next century.

Grabbing a half-empty beer bottle from last night, I wash down four ibuprofen with the warm, stale beer and flop back onto the mattress. Staring at the crack in the ceiling above my bed reminds me once again how bad this place sucks. I liked it better when Mason and I shared his dad's house, before he married Penny and had kids.

He's such a lucky bastard.

Actually, I liked it better when I was lying in bed next to Toni every morning. If that were the case, I wouldn't care where I lived. We could live in a shack or inside a cardboard box. As long as she was with me, I'd be happy.

Maybe if I would've gotten the girl that I was supposed to have had, my life would've been better too, but shit doesn't always work out the way you want it. Don't get me wrong, I'm happy for Mason, but I miss what we had when we were sharing girls after mine and Toni's breakup.

Life was so much easier back then. One of us would find a cute girl, test the waters to see if she was up for a threesome and bam! It definitely helped keep my mind off of her. I spent a lot of years numb, bedding anyone who was willing, trying to fill that empty void. It worked for a little bit, but reality would always catch back up to me.

When we shared girls, we'd share them like no tomorrow. No relationship, no strings, no commitments; there was only a promise to each other—our pact—and that was once we shared a girl, we *always* shared her.

It was a simple rule to keep feelings out of the way so that nobody got hurt, and so that it never ruined our friendship. Mason and I were always like brothers, but now that he's married, started a family, and began running his own business, things aren't the same. I don't have anyone.

It's only me.

Well, me plus Alicia, but she doesn't count. We've never entered an official relationship status, despite what she believes. She might be annoying, but at least I don't have to spend too much time alone, which is probably the only thing that's kept me from drinking myself to death.

There have been a few times when I've come close to that point. Things were real bad after I found myself suddenly single for something that I had very little decision in. It sucks to wake up in the ER after they've pumped your stomach. I know because it's happened twice in the last six years. The first time wasn't too long after Toni ceased to exist in my life, and the second time was on the one-year anniversary of the last time I saw her.

Glancing at the alarm clock beside my bottle of ibuprofen, I watch the digital numbers flip to 5:02. Right on cue, Alicia calls like she does every day when she gets off of work, but today, she's not calling to see if I want to grab a bite to eat or hang out.

"Hello?" I answer, my voice croaking as I try to ignore the jackhammers beating my brains into an oblivion.

"Lucas? Are you still in bed? You know you need to be up right now," she says.

The jackhammers ramp up their speed with each word that vibrates over the phone line.

"Yeah, I know," I run my hand through my hair as I sit up on the bed. Looking into the dresser mirror, I can see my disheveled hair sticking out all over the place. "I'm working on it."

My eyes are sunken in and the dark circles beneath them look even darker in comparison to my pale skin. That's what happens when you lose half your work and are never outside. Thanks St. Louis City PD, I think to myself.

"Your meeting starts in 90 minutes, you better get your ass up and moving." I don't respond, which pisses her off as usual when she tries to boss me around. I've always liked the girls with daddy issues because they're easier to control, but Alicia is headstrong and demands control.

Being with her is a double-edged sword. I want her in my life because it means not being lonely and I need her in my life to help keep me in line, but we're not a perfect match; not even close. I'm not sure what I'm doing with her, but we have had some pretty good times together, so I outweigh the good with the bad and deal with her because she's good for me—in a way.

The same kind of way that your mother would be good for you if you had one. Mine's been gone so long that I don't remember her voice.

"Lucas! Are you listening to me?"

I nod, even though she can't see me, "Yeah. I hear you. I'll be ready, but I don't see the point."

"The point, Lucas," she clicks her tongue off the roof of her mouth, which usually means I'm going to get an earful. "You need these meetings to get your license back so you can get your construction business back up and running at full speed." I know what she's saying is true, but I don't care anymore. Going to these meetings or getting my license back isn't going to make me stop drinking, or improve my life in some unforeseeable way. "Just get in the shower, please. I'll be there in like twenty minutes. Okay?"

"Whatever, Alicia," I sigh. "I'll see you when you get here."

Stepping under the shower head, I let the water cascade down my face and body. It feels good, but it's not enough to get me up and running at full speed. Lathering myself up, I try to scrub away the stench of alcohol so that my hangover's not so obvious when I show up to this AA meeting tonight.

As I reach for the power button on the coffee maker, I hear a knock before the front door opens. "It's just me," Alicia yells from the living room. "Lucas? Where are you?"

"In here," I call from the kitchen. "I'm making some coffee."

"Well, don't you look fab," she rolls her eyes. "What'd you do? Wake up and start drinking again? You look like shit."

"Thanks, you're gorgeous yourself," I mock her. "And no, I didn't wake up and start drinking. You called right as I was opening my eyes, and then I took a shower, and now here I am," I wave my blue coffee mug in the air.

She checks her watch. "You better hurry up with that coffee. Your meeting starts in 40 minutes, and you don't want to be late."

"Who gives a shit?" I mumble as I turn to face the coffee pot.

"Um, the person who has to sign your paper at the end of each meeting? He or she might like to know that you were in full attendance before they sign off on something for the court."

"Yeah, fuck," I mutter. "I need to find that paper."

"Lucas! Tell me you're fucking around, and that you know where your paper is," she says. "How are you going to get your life back in order if you can't even handle a sheet of paper?"

"I don't know, *mom*," I mock her. "I'll think of something."

Spinning on her heels, she heads toward my bedroom.

"Did you put it with the rest of your papers when I picked you up from jail? The ones with your court hearing and everything? I thought I saw you put them all together."

Rolling my eyes, I pour myself a cup of Joe and drink it black, hoping I can pump enough into my body before the meeting to at least take the edge off this headache.

"You can check, but I'm not sure."

I'm not worried about that paper. Alicia keeps track of little important shit like that, and, most likely, she put all the papers together. It's probably in there somewhere.

"Got it!" she yells. "Now come on, let's get out of here and get down to your meeting, and I'll keep track of this," she flicks the paper with her fingers.

"Fine by me," I say, grabbing my coat as we head out.

CHAPTER TWO

TONI

This week's meeting couldn't come fast enough for me. With all the stress that I've been going through lately, I've been craving a stiff drink, but I've stopped myself each time. It hasn't been easy, but my sobriety is worth it because I've come to realize that my life is better without the alcohol—and all the random men.

I went through a phase for a couple of years where I couldn't commit to a relationship. Nobody could ever compare to Lucas or fill his shoes, so I had a lot of casual sex. None of them mattered, but they were a distraction and they made me feel good about myself for a minute.

It almost became a contest. I'd get myself all psyched up as I painted my face and straightened my hair just before I squeezed into the tightest pair of jeans that would go over my round, bubbly ass. I'd always ask myself, "Is Toni going to nail it or strike out tonight?"

Normally, I nailed it, but it's not hard to do when you spend your weekends at various clubs and bars. That's where men flock to on the weekends, hoping to find some desperate drunk chick with an easy pussy. The only difference is that I went to the bar willing before I had a drop of alcohol. The liquor just helped me forget that I was a complete whore.

I didn't hit rock bottom until I woke up in a strange guy's house. My clothes were in a pile on the floor next to me when I opened my eyes and I was in a room by myself. I had no clue exactly where I was or who I'd gone home with, but I started freaking out when I couldn't pull the bedroom door open. I kept trying to figure out why I'd be alone in what looked like a spare bedroom. Where was the guy and why did he leave me alone?

After working on the door for about ten minutes, it finally opened. How I mustered the strength, I have no idea because I was hungover as usual, but my body felt weird. It was like I'd been drugged—and I probably was. I'd never felt like that a day in my life before that night and have never felt like it since. I was so disoriented and even though I could *watch* my body move, such as my arms or legs, I couldn't *feel* my body move.

Stepping out into the hallway, I see that I'm in some

sort of mansion. That's what it appeared to be like, anyway. The hallway was long and wide, with a set of spiraling staircases on each end of it that led to the downstairs. The black wrought iron railing looked like a refinished antique, perfectly polished. My guess is that he had a housekeeper or maid.

I don't know why, maybe call it intuition, I began tiptoeing out into the hall and started to make my way down the staircase that was closest to me. When I was within 15 feet of the front door, I heard a man speaking from sounded like the area behind the staircase.

I was very quiet and tried to listen. What I heard scared the shit out of me. I was crouched down, trying my best to hide behind the steps that offered what little shelter they could, and I saw a group of men. The one who was talking appeared to be the leader—and the owner of the house that I was in.

I heard him say, "The least I'll take for her is a million, and that's because I'm feeling generous. I sampled the goods last night after I got her home, and she's well worth three mill, but I'm offering you a discount to take her off my hands."

Bolting for the door, I practically leapt through it and fell down the front steps as I scrambled to run away. That was when I decided to get my ass to the first AA meeting that I could find and get some help.

When I pull up in front of the big brick building, I take a moment to think about how far I've come before getting out of the car and going inside. I still remember my first time coming to a meeting. I wasn't sure if I belonged here, or even how long I'd last. Everyone talked about the 12 steps, and I thought it was complete bullshit until I got serious about getting my head on straight.

Sitting in the meetings listening to everyone else's rock bottom showed me that I was no different from anyone sitting in the group. We all had our own struggles and problems, some worse than others, but there was a commonality: we all needed help.

Once I realized how badly I needed help and committed myself to becoming sober, I started working the first step. I had no clue how much harder each step would be, but when there's a will, there's a way.

I grab my bag off the seat next to me and make my way inside the building and feel the biting cold nipping at my heels as the thick, heavy door shuts behind me. The warmth of the building feels so good, especially because the heater core in my car is going out so the heat's sporadic at best—if it works at all.

This building used to be a church, but they sold it when they built a bigger, better facility just outside of the city limits. You can still smell the holy water and scented candles, though, and the maroon carpet could definitely use an upgrade.

Sliding the strap of my bag onto my shoulder, I take a deep breath and walk down the empty hallway until I hear the familiar voices from my AA meetings. Most of them have already gathered in our room.

Like clockwork, everyone's huddled around the coffee area. Mark, who heads our AA meetings, found an old table in the basement and carried it up here so we could have a coffee station. We all take turns bringing a can of coffee and help with buying creamer, sugar, and sometimes donuts. I try to stay away from them, though. Just because I quit drinking, it doesn't mean I want to gain an extra 30 pounds, so I stick to coffee with two sugars and one creamer.

"Toni!" Monica says.

She's been coming to these meetings since they started holding them here. I admire her and her strength; she was actually my sponsor for the longest time, and that's how we became very close friends. It's been a long four years, but we're going strong.

"Hey Mon," I say, giving her a hug. "How've you been?"

She smiles at me, tucking her hair behind her ear. "You know how it is, taking one day at a time."

"Same here," I say, grabbing a styrofoam cup to pour myself some coffee. "Trying anyway."

Trying is an understatement, but I know we've all got our own problems and that's why we're here. She wraps her hand around my arm and in her soft, sweet voice she says, "Tell us at the meeting. We're here to support you. I'm so proud of you."

Knowing that Monica is proud of me makes me smile. She met me at my lowest, not too long after everything happened and I hit rock bottom. It was about two years after I'd last seen Lucas and we ended things. God, I still remember it all. No amount of booze could ever make me forget. There's plenty that I don't remember while I spent those two years in a drunken stupor, but I remember how our relationship deteriorated, how it became broken, and inevitably, irreparable.

I'd rather have a knife stabbed into my back and twisted in a thousand directions rather than re-live the beginning of the end.

I was so scared, and didn't know how to tell him. We were at my apartment, sitting on the couch as we watched TV. He knew something was up and wouldn't let up until I told him what was bothering me.

"Lucas, I'm pregnant," I said.

It was my second year of college, and I knew there was no way that I could keep it. Money was too tight and I was barely making ends meet. Having a baby was out of the question.

"You're what?" he said, sitting up. He was so excited; his eyes lit right up.

"Pregnant."

Saying those words sounded foreign to me, like they weren't right. They didn't belong on my lips. I wasn't sure how Lucas would take it or what he would want me to do, but I already knew what needed to be done. It wouldn't be fair for an innocent baby to be brought into this world by someone who couldn't care for it. I could barely take care of myself.

"Are you sure? Did you take a test?"

I nodded, biting my lip. He wrapped his strong hands around my petite fingers and squeezed. "When did you find out?"

"About a week ago," I said, my voice low and cracking. We'd been together since the summer I graduated high school, and I knew he'd want me to keep it. We loved each other so much, and I thought our love could withstand anything.

"Have you made a doctor's appointment or anything? I'm not really sure what pregnant ladies do," he laughed.

He noticed that I wasn't smiling. I didn't share the same excitement that he did, not at all.

"I made an appointment at Planned Parenthood," I said quietly. "It's tomorrow."

"Planned Parenthood? I didn't know you could go there. I thought you'd have to go to a doctor."

He didn't know what I was saying, and it killed me to know that I was going to have to say it out loud to the man I loved.

"Do you know what Planned Parenthood is, or what they do there?" I asked.

"No. They give out condoms and stuff, right? Like, you can go there for birth control?"

I looked into his big brown eyes. They were so soft and sweet; loving and caring. We could party our asses off, but he was always so loving toward me.

"They do those things," I slowed my words and spoke very carefully. "And they also do abortions."

His smile quickly disappeared and his grip on my hand relaxed. "An abortion? Is that what you want to do?"

It was never what I **wanted** to do, but it was what I **needed** to do. After a long talk with many shed tears, he agreed to go with me to the clinic the next day for my consult.

"Is everyone almost ready?" Mark says as he adds a few more chairs to our group.

The group mumbles an unanimous, "Yes," as I finish stirring my coffee and take a sip.

"Come on," Monica says, pulling my arm. "We'll sit next to each other."

The warm liquid feels good going down as it begins to warm my insides, so I take another swig, hoping to maximize the warmth. We're all taking a seat when a couple, a man and woman, enters the room, and I nearly choke to death on my coffee.

It's Lucas with some woman.

I want to run and hide. I can't deal with him today, but the moment I think about excusing myself from the meeting, we lock eyes. He spots me straight away, and the two of us stare at one another for what seems like an eternity. A thousand unspoken words pass between us before the woman he's with grabs his arm and drags him to a set of chairs just a few spaces away from Mon and me.

"Are you okay?" she turns to me as I shift in my seat.

"Yeah, I'm good," I lie.

My body has this fleeting urge to jump out of my chair and hit the door, but I know it'll cause a scene so I stay put as I wonder why he's here. Is he there to support her? Is she there to support him? Do they both have a drinking problem?

Does God just hate me?

I can't believe that he's here with another woman—not that I expected him to stay single, but it hurts like hell to know that he's moved on. I never really did.

Instead, I went into a downward spiral of depression, which landed me here, but I'm recovering. I'm taking steps to improve my life, but the moment I see him, I know it could all come undone.

"Who would like to begin today?" Mark asks as he begins the meeting, breaking my concentration as he pulls me back into reality.

CHAPTER THREE

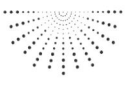

LUCAS

The second I step foot in the room, I spot Toni. I want to turn around and leave, but Alicia has a firm grip on my arm, dragging me closer to the meeting that I didn't want to come to in the first place. Seeing Toni makes me want to scramble to get out of here as fast as I can.

Everything in my chest begins to hurt and I can feel my heart pounding in my eardrums as every sound in the room begins to fade away. I try everything I can to not look at her, but my eyes are drawn to her like a duck to water.

I try to tell myself that these meetings are only temporary, but it doesn't make my anxiety any better. In fact, it makes it worse. What if she's at every meeting and I have to see her each week that I'm here? Or worse: what if we never speak?

"I'd like to go first," a woman says, as Alicia and I take a seat just a few chairs from Toni.

"That'd be great. We have some new faces here tonight, so I'd like for everyone to do a brief introduction," the man in charge of the meeting says. "I'm Mark and I've been holding these meetings for the last twelve years."

The woman smiles, and I can see she's missing a few of her front teeth. She looks like she's in her early 50's, but my guess is she's probably in her 40's. Drugs and drinking have a way of wearing a person's youth away, and she looks like she's lived a hard life.

"I'm Frenchy," she begins. "And I've been a recovering alcoholic for almost two years. The past week has been tough for me because I've been trying really hard to get a job. My sister's been on my ass, you know?" Everyone nods in agreement. "She doesn't understand how hard it is for someone like us to get a job. I can't always be perfect like her."

"Do you have any leads, Frenchy?" Mark asks.

"I thought I did. Last week, I went on two interviews. One of the places said they would make a decision by yesterday, but I never heard back from them." She frowns and wipes away a tear. "I guess I didn't get the job."

"It's okay, Frenchy, you'll get the next one and it'll

probably be better. Remember, sometimes we 'miss opportunities' because there's a bigger plan in store for us," Mark says. "Who'd like to go next?"

"I will," the woman beside Toni stands up. "My name is Monica, but everyone calls me Mon. This past week was filled with its ups and downs. As most of you know, I've been trying to repair my relationship with my daughter, and it hasn't gone very well, but I think we're finally starting to make some progress. After a big argument that we had, we both apologized and she invited me over to her house for dinner this weekend so I can meet her new boyfriend."

"That's fantastic, Mon. Are there any problems you'd like to discuss?" he asks her.

"No, I just hope my higher power grants me the strength to make it through dinner with her. When I've gone over to her house in the past, we tend to argue, but I'm willing to give it another shot. She only started talking to me about a year ago, so I expect rough patches."

As everyone goes around the circle, I realize that hearing their stories makes me want to drink more, not less. I can't believe I have to put up with this shit for the next three months just so I can get my license back. If it weren't for that judge mandating I get the stupid paper signed, I would've been out of here a long time ago.

The only reason that I'm still sitting in this chair is

because Alicia won't let me leave, and I hope to find some way to connect with Toni. I want to know what she has to say and why she's here or what she's doing with her life.

Almost an hour later, it's my turn to talk and I'm nervous as hell. I'm not one to talk about my problems, nor do I do confessions. Mark looks straight at me, "Would you like to go next?"

Clearing my throat, I stand up and quickly scan the circle. Toni's eyes meet mine for a brief second before her eyelids flutter and she focuses on her shoes. It kills me to see her here, she looks so sad, and maybe a little angry.

"I, um, my name's Lucas. I'm here because the judge ordered I get my paper signed and successfully complete AA to get my license back."

Nodding, I go to take my seat, but Mark stops me. "Lucas, we're glad you're here. Would you say that you have a drinking problem?"

Toni's eyes find mine again and, this time, she waits for my answer. Looking into her eyes, I say, "I guess you could say that."

She is the reason why I started drinking and going out partying all the time. She's the whole reason why I can't commit to relationships or get close to anyone. What happened between us is something I've never been able to get over. I never wanted her to have that abortion, but I couldn't make her see things any other way, so I did what any good man would do. I supported her decision because I thought it was better than forcing her into doing something she didn't want to do and ruining our relationship forever, but things didn't work out anyway.

"What brought you here?" he asks me. I look around and see that everyone's staring at me. I feel like I'm on trial or something. Drawing in a deep breath, I exhale slowly as I think about why I'm here.

"I had a few too many DUI's and, as a result, I lost my license. My construction business is in jeopardy because of it, and I just want to get things back on the right track."

I'm embarrassed and ashamed to admit this but know that she's sitting in the same room listening makes it ten times worse. I feel like a loser and I never want her to think of me that way.

Mark nods, "You've certainly come to the right place. We've all been where you are. I assume this is your first AA meeting?"

"Yeah," I shake my head. "Something like that."

I've looked into counseling and AA meetings before, but I was too embarrassed to reach out for help. The judge made that decision for me, though.

"How long have you had a drinking problem?"

I look at Toni, who has gone back to staring at her

shoes. She won't even look at me as I continue to talk, and it feels like a knife is twisting deep inside my gut. "About six years, I'd say."

That gets her attention and her head shoots straight up as she looks right at me. There's a look of recognition in her eyes; maybe that's when her problems started too—right after we split up.

It's hard to say what would've happened between us, but I would've married that girl if we could've worked through our problems. I loved her more than the air that I breathed and if given the choice between loving her or breathing, I would've used my last breath to tell her how much I loved her.

"Thank you, Lucas," he says, motioning for me to take my seat. "Who's left?"

As I sit back down in my chair, Alicia grabs hold of my arm and squeezes it. "You did great," she whispers.

I know she means well, but her words don't offer me much comfort. I'm ready to get out of here and go have a drink but knowing her, she's not going to let me out of her sight.

Everyone looks at each other as we wait to see who's turn it is to talk next before Mark says, "Toni? How about you? You haven't gone yet."

Pushing her chair back, she stands and smoothes her

hair back as a weak smile spreads across her face. My mind races, wondering what she'll say. Will her story match mine? Or will it be something completely different? Sitting in my chair, I hold my breath until she begins talking, unable to move a muscle.

CHAPTER FOUR

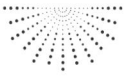

TONI

Hearing Lucas's story shocked the hell out of me. I had no idea that he'd taken the same path as me once we called it quits. Obviously, everything went downhill for him at the same time it did for me; he said six years ago and looked straight at me. It hurt so bad to hear him say that.

Everything is my fault. I fucked it all up—for both of us. He must think I'm the worst person in the world after everything we went through.

I know this sounds terrible, but part of me felt a little better knowing that he couldn't easily get over me and that we both went through the same struggles because I know I'm not alone. I felt so selfish for the longest time, but knowing that it hurt him as much as it hurt me brings me some sort of relief that it wasn't all in my head. We had a really good thing, and there were so many times that I wondered how he was.

I can't count the days when I wondered what he was doing or where he was at, or if he was thinking of me.

But the other part of me is sad that he dealt with things alone. It's never easy to hear that someone you once loved and cared about went down such a dark path.

The fact that he's barely holding on to his dad's construction business tells me a lot. When we were together, he still worked for his dad, but I guess his dad handed it down to him. That business meant everything to him and his dad, and the fact that he's let things get this far out of hand shows me that maybe our relationship affected him more than I could've imagined.

I'm assuming the woman who's with him is only here for moral support since she didn't speak or introduce herself. She must care for him a lot because nobody comes to these things voluntarily, at least not at first. I find myself wondering how long the two of them have been together and whether she's an enabler or not. I guess it's really none of my business.

"I'm Toni," I say, quickly introducing myself. "I've been attending these meetings for the past four years and Mon," I glance down at her, "has been my sponsor most of that time."

She smiles up at me and nods, "Sure have, and I wouldn't trade it for the world."

"My last week has been hectic," I admit. "And I wanted to take a load off, but I didn't. I stayed clean. Every time I thought about stopping off for a drink on my way home, I called Mon and talked to her until I was in for the night."

"What happened last week, Toni? How's your laundromat business going?" Mark asks.

A short laugh escapes my throat. "Not good. I just got all of the inspections finished and found out that the bank loan will barely cover any of the repairs that I need to make in order to get the building up to code. It's going to cost a fortune."

"Are there any grants that you could take advantage of? A lot of times the government will give small business owner grants to help get things up and running."

Shifting my weight onto my other foot, I sweep my hair away from my face. "I tried, but I don't qualify for most of them. I seriously wonder if anyone actually qualifies for those things."

"So what's your plan?" Mark asks.

According to him, we must always have a plan; a safety net to fall back on.

"I don't really have one at the moment," I bite my lip. "But I'm working on it. I have an appointment with the bank manager on Friday to see if I can get a small loan. According to the inspection reports, it shouldn't cost me more than ten grand to fix the plumbing and the gas leak that's inside the building. If I would've known the building had so many issues, I would've never bought it."

"Do you think you'll get the loan?" he asks.

I shrug, "Your guess is as good as mine. I barely got the business loan to buy the laundromat, but I'm hoping they'll say yes. I just got my credit cards paid off last month, so I'm hoping that'll shoot up my credit score."

"Well, it sounds like you have a plan," Mark says. "You've come a long way, but it sounds like you're moving in the right direction."

Before the meeting is over, Mark talks about working the twelve steps and how much of an impact they can make if you stay the course. His voice drowns out to nothing but background noise as I study Lucas and his girlfriend. She seems more tentative to what's going on in the meeting than he does, by far.

After hearing his story and watching him, I can see that he's only here because he has to be, and not because he wants to be. If he's serious about changing his life or keeping his business, it's vital that he works the twelve steps regardless what the judge has ordered or he'll be right back in the same boat.

I realize that the meeting is over when everyone

stands up, and quickly scramble to my feet to join them. As soon as we say our goodbyes, I snatch my purse from the floor and leave as quickly as possible. The last thing I want is to look like I'm lingering or waiting around for him.

In the parking lot, I hear Mon calling my name.

"Toni!" she yells. "Wait up!" Running toward my car, she bends over, catching her breath as she rests her hands on her knees. "How come you took off like that?"

Glancing at the door, I make sure Lucas and his girlfriend are nowhere around. "You know the new guy that was in the meeting?" She nods, still out of breath. "That's *him*."

"Him? Him, who?"

"The guy that I told you about." Her face twists in confusion. "The one who I had the abortion with and everything crumbled after that?" I jog her memory.

"Oh! Oh, shit!" she says. "Are you going to talk to him? Or do you not want to talk to him?"

"I can't talk to him," I say. "Besides, he's clearly moved on and has a girlfriend and everything."

"Remember step eight?" she says, in a low, sweet voice. "You need to make amends. You two went through a lot together, and it seems like you're both hurting."

"Remember step nine?" I counter. "You only make amends if it won't harm the other person. I think talking to him would do more harm than good. Like I said, it seems like he has support. I don't want to ruin anything. I remember being here even though I didn't want to, and if he were here to confront me at my first meeting, I don't think I would've come back. It's better if I just leave things be and let him work on his recovery at his own will."

"Do whatever your heart tells you to do," she takes my hand in hers. "You're a good person, Toni, and I know you'll do the right thing."

"Thanks, Mon. I better get going. I'll see you around."

She wraps her arms around me, giving me a firm hug. "Call if you need anything. Not only have I been your sponsor for the last few years, but I'm also your best friend."

"I know," I open my car door. "I'm going to get out of here before they come out. We'll talk later."

I fire up my engine and begin to back out of the parking space just as Lucas and his girlfriend walk out of the building. Whew, I think to myself, bullet dodged, but I doubt he even saw me, even though I couldn't stop staring at him.

CHAPTER FIVE

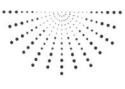

LUCAS

After getting my paper signed by Mark, Alicia and I head out of the building. Even though I made it through the first bullshit meeting, I know there are many more to come. I dread it and welcome it at the same time if it means getting to hear her speak at each of the meetings.

I'm dying to know as much about her as humanly possible. I've worried about her so many times over the years, but I was too scared to call her or go by her place. I laugh to myself at being too scared. What man the size of me could possibly be afraid of tiny Toni?

It's not so much that I'm afraid of her, but afraid of her rejection. It's possible that it would literally kill me if she rejected me. There's no way I could take it. It'd probably be enough to push me off the deep end.

"I could really use a drink after listening to everyone else's problems," I say to Alicia.

"How about if we grab something to eat instead? You can't drink if you're going to clean up your act," she says. Rolling my eyes at her, I know she's right and I hate it. "We'll get Chinese takeout on the way home."

"Whatever," I mumble.

During the car ride, I can't stop thinking about how Toni bought a business. She was never the entrepreneur type, but I'm glad to know that she was able to turn over a new leaf after everything that happened. It gives me a bit of hope that if she can do it, so can I.

She's always had a good head on her shoulders and very intelligent. It was just a few of the qualities that attracted me to her in the first place. Toni's not like any other girl I've ever met before, and that's what makes her so special.

I can't help but wonder why she'd buy a laundromat of all things. Why not a coffee shop, a donut shop, a bakery, or something else? There's only one laundromat that I can think of that'd be for sale and it's the one off of Grand and Gravois. It's not the best neighborhood, and everyone around there relies on that place. From what I can remember, it shut down about six months ago, so she must've taken ownership of it very recently.

"Hello? Earth to Lucas," Alicia shakes my arm. "We're here. Are you coming in to order with me?"

Snapping out of my thoughts, I look around and see that we're parked in front of the Chinese restaurant. "Yeah, sorry. I was just thinking."

We get out of the car and begin walking inside. "What were you thinking about?" She asks.

"Those stupid meetings. One down, eleven more to go," I say, opening the door for her.

"Yeah? Well, those 'stupid meetings' are only once a week, and I think they're going to change your life."

I laugh at the thought of them changing my life. "I don't know about all that, but they will help me get my license back so that I don't have to worry about driving illegally anymore."

We step up to the counter and order our usual dinner combos of sweet and sour chicken with chicken fried rice before we sit down and wait for them to cook our food.

"I know," she says as we take a seat. "That worries the hell out of me. Do you know how much trouble you could get into if you got caught driving without your license?"

"Don't do this, Alicia. I have to go to work, I have bills to pay." I'm tired of her always lecturing me.

"Lucas, if you get caught driving on a suspended license, you could lose it for good. Then what? You'll still keep driving, right?"

"Well, I'll still keep eating, so yeah, I don't really have a choice. Do I?"

"When will you stop living on the edge?" Her voice is weary.

"Probably never," I reply.

The woman behind the counter calls out our order, saving me from another tiring argument with Alicia.

We eat dinner in complete silence as we watch TV. Calling it an early night, I say, "Guess I better get to bed soon. I have to work in the morning."

Removing our dishes from the table, Alicia cleans up as our show is ending. "Where are you working tomorrow?"

I don't want to talk about it because I'm not proud of what my work has dwindled to. "I have to repair a couple of basement walls," I answer.

My construction company went from doing jobs all over the area for big name companies to repairing basement walls of homeowners. Work has been tough lately and with being limited to where I can accept jobs, I've been taking anything I can get.

"Oh? Well, how about if I stay the night tonight? I'll keep you company."

I don't have the heart to kick her out. I'd prefer alone time to process everything, but I know she'll be offended if I say no. "Sure," I reply. "Whatever suits you."

As we lie in bed, I can't get Toni out of my mind. She looked so damn good. The way her coffee-colored brown hair framed her face brought out her beautiful cocoa brown eyes and her high cheek bones. It seems like it's been forever since I laid eyes on her, and she's even more beautiful than I remember her.

She seemed happy, despite whatever's going on with her laundromat. I'm happy for her, even though I miss her like crazy. I'd pick her over any woman, but I doubt she'd waste a second thought thinking about me.

I noticed that she didn't wait around at the end of the meeting to get a paper signed like I did, so I bet she's going on her own free will. She's always been so much stronger than I ever have when it comes to doing the right things.

Drifting off to sleep, I wrap my arm around Alicia as I secretly pretend it's Toni. She's all I ever wanted, and now that I've seen her, I can't stop thinking about her.

It's still dark outside when I wake up, and Alicia's sprawled out in bed next to me. Her pale leg is a reminder that she's not Toni, and I hate myself for not trying harder when I had a chance to make things right between us.

"Good morning," a lazy smile plays on Alicia's lips. "Are you getting up for work?"

Running my hand through my hair, I throw my legs over the edge of the bed. "Yep, it appears so."

"I'll join you in the shower," she giggles.

The last thing I want is her in the shower with me, but she's determined as hell to join me anyway. "It's okay. I have to make it quick so I get there on time."

"Babe," she whines. "Let me take a shower with you. I'll put on some coffee while you get the water heated up."

Sighing, I get out of bed and turn on the water, hopeful that I'll get in and out before she has a chance to jump in with me. Washing the suds out of my hair, I'm almost done when I hear the curtain clink open.

"Hey, babe," she stands before me in all her naked glory.

She has a smoking hot body, but I'm not interested this morning. All I can think about is Toni. I dreamt of her all night and replayed one of our last fights over and over. It was the day we went to the clinic—a day I'll never forget.

"Are you sure you want to do this?" I asked her as we sat in the waiting room. It's not too late if you want to change your mind."

She looked up from the magazine she was pretending to read. "I'm sure."

"We can make this work if you want to keep it. I'll do whatever needs to be done."

"Lucas! Stop it," she hissed. Suspicious eyes casted upon us from everyone in the room. "We're doing this."

We sat in silence until the called her name.

"Toni Summers," the nurse appeared with a clipboard. "Come on back."

I followed her to the room where she dressed in a paper gown and put her feet in the stirrups.

The dream stopped at that point, and I woke up every damned time. I think it's because my mind won't let me think about what happened next. Reliving the next part is a nightmare, and it's something that still haunts me to this day. We could've had a family together, and I meant it when I told her I'd do everything possible to make sure that she was taken care of—her and the baby.

"Hey," my voice croaks as Alicia joins me in the shower.

Without another word, she steps in beside me and immediately gets on her knees. "Let me help you make sure you're *extra* clean."

Before I can stop her, her hand is around the base of my cock and her warm tongue is swirling around the tip. Looking down, I see her wide eyes close shut as she takes my entire length in her mouth and hums as she alternates sucking and stroking my shaft.

"Fuck," I mumble, the hot water hitting my back.

With a loud pop, she takes my dick out of her mouth and smiles up at me. "That's right, baby. Let me take care of you today."

Deep throating my cock, I close my eyes and imagine it's Toni. The problem is, Toni was way better at giving head, but Alicia's determined to get me off before I go to work.

Reaching up with her free hand, she cups my balls and sucks even harder, swirling her tongue around every rigid vein my cock has to offer. Eager to make me come, she uses the warm water as lubrication for my cock and begins stroking it. I close my eyes and picture Toni wearing her black leggings and high-heeled boots with her form fitting blouse from the meeting last night, and that's all I need to give me that final push.

My load starts shooting out, all over Alicia's face and chest. Smiling, she admires her handiwork and continues stroking me until she's completely drained my balls.

CHAPTER SIX

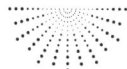

TONI

"What's the damage?" I ask the gas man as he finalizes his estimate.

Holding his clipboard, he let's out a long, low whistle. "You have a couple of options. There's a quick fix and there's the right way. Which one do you prefer?"

"Tell me both of my options," I say, taking the clipboard from his hands.

"Doing things the right way is going to cost you about six grand."

I frown at the thought of spending six grand to repair the gas leak. "What's the quick fix?" I ask.

"Light a match."

"Shit. That bad, huh?"

"I'm afraid so. As bad as it is, I'm surprised this place hasn't already blown."

"So what do I do now?"

"Nothing. I've got the gas turned off until you get it fixed."

"Shut off?" I ask. "You can't just shut me off! How am I supposed to have hot water or heat?"

"Listen, lady, it's not my problem. Get it fixed and we'll turn it back on. Okay?"

I purse my lips at him. "Any suggestions on who I should call?"

He digs in the breast pocket of his shirt and pulls out a stack of business cards. Sorting through them, he hands me one. "These guys ought to be able to handle it, but they're always booked, so I don't know how fast they'll be able to get you in."

"Thanks," I say.

"Yep, have a good one." He grabs his bag and makes his way out the door, letting it slam shut as he leaves.

One of the ceiling tiles springs open, causing some of the insulation to come tumbling down. "Just great," I mutter. Cleaning up the mess, a man wearing white overalls walks in.

"Can I help you?" I ask.

"Are you," he looks at his paperwork, "Toni Summers?"

"I am," I shake his hand.

"I'm Matt. You called about an estimate on getting the walls repaired?"

Looking around the place, I note all of the peeling and dilapidated drywall that's seemingly coming apart. I can't afford anymore repairs, but I have to get this place up to code and looking better. "Yeah," I say, frowning again. "Can you make it quick? I have to get to an appointment."

I'm scheduled to meet the bank manager in under an hour and I don't want to be late. Hopefully, I can make a good enough impression that he'll approve me for a big enough loan that I can get this place up and running before I'm completely broke.

Cleaning up the mess from the ceiling, I impatiently wait as Matt walks around checking the walls and taking notes on his findings. I glance at my watch, and see that I only have 20 minutes to get to the bank.

"Are you almost finished?" I ask, emptying a dustpan full of insulation into the trash.

"From what I can tell, these walls have to be completely gutted. Not only is the drywall bad, but the wooden beams need to be replaced."

"What? Why?" I ask.

"Looks like this place once had termites, and nobody ever repaired the walls. Once an infestation gets this bad and you add the age of the building, it's only a matter of time before you have to tear it all down to rebuild it."

"Jesus," I shiver as the temperature in the building drops a few more degrees since the gas man shut off the heat. "What's that going to cost?"

"I'd say about three thousand dollars."

"That's it? Only three grand to redo the walls?" I'm a bit surprised that it's cheaper to gut the walls than it is to repair the gas line.

"No," he laughs, shaking his head. "For one wall. We'll have to redo all of the walls in here, plus the three in the back."

I quickly start doing the math, and my jaw drops. "That's $21,000! Why is it so much?"

He rips off a sheet of paper from his notepad. "The materials will cost you about $16,000, and then about $5,000 for labor." He hands me the paper so I can see the breakdown of the estimate. "But we can just focus on the walls in here to get you started, since this is the bones of the laundromat. That'll only cost about $15,000."

All of these numbers are making my head spin, and I can't deal with it right now. "I'll give you a call. Right now, I've got to get down to the bank to see about taking out a loan to cover some of the cost of this."

"No problem. You can just give me a call when you're ready, and we'll get you put on the schedule."

"Thanks," I say, walking him to the door, locking up as we make our way out onto the sidewalk. "I'll let you know."

On my way to the bank, I run the numbers in my head again just to make sure I'm not crazy. All in all, it sounds like I'll need close to $30,000 to get the gas leak repaired and get the walls redone.

Making my way into the bank, I do my best to straighten my hair from the wind and have a seat across from the bank manager's desk as I wait for him to finish up with his current client.

"Ms. Summers?" he calls my name.

"Yes, right here," I get out of my seat and make my way to his desk. "Thank you so much for seeing me today."

"It's my pleasure," he shakes my hand. "How's the new business going?"

Taking a seat, I cross my legs and clear my throat. "That's what I wanted to talk to you about. I'm going to need another loan—a smaller one to cover some repairs before I can get it up and running."

The deep lines in his forehead crinkle as he pulls my files up on the computer. He takes his sweet time looking at the numbers and re-runs my credit. "How much are we talking?" he asks.

"I'd like to take out another thirty-thousand," I say as

he narrows his eyes at me and pushes his glasses up on the bridge of his nose. "But I've paid off some other debts, which has, hopefully, improved my credit score and decreased my income-to-debt ratio."

Smoothing his silver hair, he leans back in his chair and places his finger on his lip as he continues to stare at the computer screen. "Your income to debt ratio?" He laughs. "I'm sorry, Toni, but you don't have any income at this point."

"But what about my savings, or my waitressing job? Surely, that has to count for something, and as soon as I have the laundromat up and running, my income will be better. I just have to get over this hurdle to get the repairs made."

He studies my face for a moment. "Toni, I'm going to ask you a serious question, and I need a serious answer." I nod and swallow the lump in my throat. "Didn't you get the building inspected before you purchased it?"

I didn't and I know I should have, but the price was so cheap that I bought it without knowing what I was getting in to. "No," I say, my voice cracking. "I didn't."

"Is there any way you can do some of the work yourself to save on some of the cost?" he asks. "Because with what I'm looking at right now, the most I can lend you is about $10,000, and even that's pushing it."

"I'll take it, and see what I can do with it. I might be

able to get some help with things," I lie. The best I might be able to do is ask a couple of my friends is they'd be willing to pitch in. It shouldn't be too hard to gut the place; rebuilding it is a whole different story.

Maybe I could get my ex, David, to help me. I hate to ask him for anything, but he used to work for the gas company and knows a thing or two about fixing that type of stuff. He might charge me, but I bet it wouldn't be anything close to six thousand.

"Are you sure?" he says, crossing his arms as he leans across his desk. His breath smells like a toilet. "Because there's not much sense in taking out a loan if it's not going to be enough. It'll only throw you further into debt, and you'll start accruing interest on, yet, another loan."

"It'll be fine," I say. "Trust me. I can rip the place apart myself and use the money to purchase the materials and have some friends help me."

Or watch YouTube to see how to hang drywall, whatever. I'm not going to tell him that, though, because he'll think I'm crazy for trying to do it myself.

"If you say so," he says, printing out some documents. "I'll just need to get your John Hancock on these papers and then I'll deposit the money into your checking around. It'll be a three-year loan, payments are due on the first of every month," he slides the papers across the desk for me to sign. "The interest rate will be 5.5%, and the first payment will be due in approximately 40 days from today."

Staring at the documents, I begin to wonder if I'm making the right choice, but honestly, what other choice do I really have? I've already purchased the laundromat, I can't let it just sit there.

Smiling, I make eye contact with him. "That'll be just fine."

I'm completely screwed if I can't pull all this off, but I know I'll kick myself in the ass if I don't at least give it a shot.

CHAPTER SEVEN

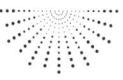

LUCAS

Sitting around the house is killing me. I've only worked three out of the last five business days, and adding a weekend into the mix didn't help. I'm going insane with boredom.

A man can only take so much political news and True Crime re-runs. I'm fairly certain that I've seen all of the crime shows that have been produced to date. Even though I keep watching them, I still have to wonder how these people think they can get away with kidnapping and murder. It's only common sense that you're going to get caught one way or another with how advanced science and technology are in today's world.

The only way you could get away with it thirty or more years ago was if you could outsmart the police, but even then, a lot of guys still got caught. It's nothing I'd ever have to worry about because I'm not crazy, but the shows keep me a bit entertained.

Lately, all I've thought about is Toni. I can't get her out of my mind. There's this little piece of me that won't shut up that keeps wondering if she's been thinking about me too. In a way, I hope that she has been but at the same time, I don't. I don't ever want her to be as miserable and lonely as me. I keep replaying our meeting over and over in my head, thinking about how she looked, how she spoke, and every word that she said.

It's like a TV show stuck on repeat. You just keep watching the same thing over and over again, but you can't change the channel because you wonder if you might've missed anything. I wish I could've read more into her words, but she had on her poker face. It was impossible to know what she was thinking at all.

Staring out the window, I watch the cold November rain fall. It's been a while since it's gotten this cold this early in November, but we're due for it. The last two winters have been pretty mild, which worked out in my favor since I had plenty of work lined up then. Now I just sit in my house, cruising the services section on Craigslist while I look for odd jobs to do.

There hasn't been much online lately, so I decide to call Mason to see if he needs any help with flipping any houses. He's done quite well for himself since he quit working construction with me. I see his signs in plenty of yards all across the St. Louis area, and his houses seem to sell fast. It doesn't surprise me; he's always done a great job at fixing things up.

Grabbing my phone, I scroll through my contacts until I find his name and hit send.

"What's up, Lucas?" Mason answers the phone.

"Not much. Are you busy?"

"That depends on why you're asking," he says, grunting as he slams down something heavy.

"I don't have any work at the moment and I'm going stir crazy. Could you use a hand?"

He laughs as he tries to catch his breath. "Yeah, I could definitely use some help today. I'll text you the address."

As soon as we hang up, my phone pings with an address that's not more than ten minutes from the house. Sliding on my work clothes, I grab my boots and coat before I hit the door. Pulling up in front of the house, all I see is his work truck parked on the street. I study the house and can't believe that he's working this job alone. The house is at least 80 years old, and it's in complete shambles.

Walking up the porch steps, the second stair from the top feels like it's about to cave any second. From the front stoop, I can see Mason up on a ladder, scraping the ceiling.

"Oh, you're just in time," he says as I walk into the house. "I was just about to remove this light fixture. Come give me a hand."

The house is freezing, but he has a small space heater hooked up in the living room which warms all of the ten feet surrounding it.

"Why are you working solo today?" I ask as I take the light cover from him and set it on the floor.

"My helper called in sick. Him and his wife just had a baby, so I think he's playing hooky. How come you're not working today?"

Walking over by the space heater, I try to warm up. "No work," I answer.

"Yeah? I've driven past your place almost every day for the last couple of weeks while I've been working on this house, and your truck is outside most of the time. Has it been slow?"

I hate to tell him about my DUI's and my AA meetings, but I decide to because it's better than looking like a loser who can't get jobs.

"I've had to cut back on work. I got into some trouble and my license is suspended right now," I say.

"Do you know how much trouble you could get into if you got caught driving?" he stops what he's doing to look at me.

"Yeah, thanks, Alicia. She tells me that all the time," I shake my head. "But I've got to eat, so I've got to work, you know?"

"Why'd they suspend your license?" he climbs down off the ladder.

"DUI's, but I can get it back in a few months. The judge is making me take AA meetings and as long as the guy running them signs my paperwork every week, they'll reinstate it."

Scratching the back of his neck, he shakes his head at me. "AA meetings, huh? I bet you're loving those."

"The meetings aren't so bad," I lie. "It's seeing Toni at them that makes them so damn hard."

He shoots his glance toward me, "Toni? *Your* Toni?"

I nod and curl my lips. "Yep, the one and only."

"Wow, I would've never guessed her to be at one of those things. Have you talked to her?"

I laugh as I pull off my coat and grab the other ladder to help him finish scraping the ceiling. "No, I stayed far away from her, or maybe she stayed away from me. She practically darted out of the damn place as soon as the meeting was over while I was getting my paper signed."

He wipes the sweat from his brow. "Would you have talked to her if she would've waited around?"

"Probably not, but Alicia was with me anyway. It would've been pretty awkward."

"I think you should talk to her, Lucas. You two have a lot of unfinished business."

He's right, but I hate to admit it. She was the best thing I ever had and I lost her. She meant everything to me, and, for some reason, she still does even though we live in two completely different worlds.

"I don't know about all that," I say, climbing down from the ladder.

"Why? Because of Alicia?" he stops what he's doing and stares a hole right through me. "If you ask me, you and her don't have anything in common and aren't going anywhere. I'm not sure why you're with her anyway."

"I'm not 'with' her," I throw up finger quotes for emphasis. "She just kind of hangs around. Besides, if it weren't for her helping me, I probably would've dug an even deeper hole and lost my construction business for good. At least right now it's just a temporary set back."

Climbing off the ladder, he joins me near the heater to warm up for a few minutes. "Lucas, I'm your best friend and I know you better than anyone else. You should talk to Toni."

The ceiling is completely free of paint and ready to be worked on. "What are we doing next?" I ask, changing the subject.

A chuckle escapes from his throat. "I've got about 40

sheets of drywall that need to be carried in." He pauses, "Since you're trying to change the topic of conversation."

Pulling my gloves out of my pocket, I slide them onto my hands as I ignore his snide remark. "Come on, let's go get those sheets off the truck before we freeze to death."

We work long and hard until the sky changes to a glowing darkness illuminated by the moon and we're both starved.

"Thanks for helping me out today," he reaches into his back pocket. "How does a hundred bucks sound?"

"No," I push his hand away. "I'm not taking your money. You've got a family to support and I needed something to do today before I drove myself crazy."

"Oh yeah?" A wide smile creeps across his face. "I'll keep you in mind next time I need some help. I love free labor."

"Thanks, asshole," I punch him in the arm. "Seriously, man, if you need help don't hesitate to call me. Chances are that I'm not working at the moment—at least for the next few months."

"Will do," he says. "Have a good one, and take my advice."

I don't say a word as I hop down the porch steps two at a time, but there's no way I can take his advice. What am I supposed to do? I can't just approach her out of nowhere with nothing to talk about. If she doesn't already think I'm a loser, she will at that point.

As I'm getting into my truck to drive back home, my text alert goes off with a message from Alicia. "Where are you? I'm at your place, but you're not here. I've got dinner for us."

The thought of dinner makes my mouth water as my stomach grumbles. As much as she smothers me, I'm grateful for her thoughtfulness. Mason is right, though. The two of us aren't going anywhere and never will.

Alicia is too independent and has a strong will. We're too much alike in that aspect, and I want a girl who needs me and depends on me. Alicia's not that girl.

CHAPTER EIGHT

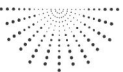

TONI

I don't know why I'm so nervous about calling David to ask for his help fixing the gas line, but my stomach is in knots. We haven't spoken since he was arrested for shoving me onto the sidewalk in front of the bar. I wish he would've just been one of the random guys that I hooked up with instead of one that I tried having a relationship with because it was the worst.

I'm not sure why he blames me, though. Nobody told him to put his hands on me, and I sure as hell didn't call the police on him. I'd thought about it a time or two when we'd get into our little spats, but I was always afraid of what he'd do to me if he found out that I called.

David had a way of communicating with anger and rage, which is why we didn't last long. The two of us only lived together for about 10 months. When he'd get pissed off, he'd push or shove me, or sometimes slap me in the face. If we were at home, he'd tear the whole place apart.

One night we were fighting about dinner because I was hungry and he was broke. I thought the simple solution would be that I'd buy dinner, but he said that the man is supposed to pay. While that may be true, my stomach wouldn't know the difference in who paid for the meal.

We went to Dairy Queen and each got a chicken strip basket. While we were sitting at home eating, we started arguing again. He decided that he wasn't going to eat anything that I paid for, so he proceeded into the kitchen to throw his food in the trash, which, no doubt, pissed me off.

As he was making his way to the trash can, I did the only thing I could think to do because all I could see was red, and I threw a chicken strip at him. I shouldn't have done it because that got him riled up, but looking back, it's kind of funny.

The chicken strip smacked him right in the back of his fat neck and made a *thwack* sound. He stopped dead in his tracks and raised his shoulders. Part of me wanted to laugh my ass off, but the other part thought, "Oh shit. What have I done?"

It sent him into a fit of rage. He flipped over the coffee

table, punched out all of our picture frames, and called me every name in the book. Things got so ugly that I ended up leaving. I didn't have any place to go, but I needed to be away from him before he put his hands on me. He'd thrown me up against a door once before this, so I knew he wasn't above touching me.

 I fled our apartment and hopped into my car, unsure as to where I was going. I started driving and after a few minutes, I decided to go hang out with two of my cousins. We're all around the same age, but they always felt like big brothers to me, and I knew they'd keep me safe from whatever David might have up his sleeve.

 After a few hours, David hadn't texted or called, so I decided to go home. He'd finally calmed down and had started cleaning some of the mess he'd made. Things continued to get progressively worse until the night we were out in front of The Cat's Meow, a bar on the Southside.

 We'd both been drinking pretty heavily, and we'd gotten into it. There was a guy at the bar, who didn't know I was with someone, and he'd offered to buy me a drink. David had a few too many shots—his liquid courage—and swore up and down that I knew this guy. It didn't stop there, though.

 According to David, not only did I know the guy, but I

must've been fucking him, too. I'd never seen this stranger a day in my life, but I couldn't convince him differently. The two of us started arguing loud enough that the bartender asked us to leave.

We barely made it out onto the sidewalk when he decided to shove me. Falling to the ground, my purse flew off my shoulder and everything came tumbling out of my bag. While I was trying to pick up my things, he used his foot to push me onto the ground again. I began yelling at him, and it was about five minutes later when the cops showed up.

That was the last night that we were a couple. I couldn't deal with him or his shit anymore. The cops took him to jail and I called his sister, and told her to come get his clothes.

After that, I decided that I wasn't getting into anymore committed relationships and found that Tinder and alcohol made quite the team. That's when things really started to unravel for me.

Meaningless sex and alcohol was all I needed to numb myself from the harsh reality that I'd pushed the only man away from me who meant the world to me. It was far too late to go back and try to fix things, so I let them be.

It was easier that way.

Tapping the call button, I hope he answers, and he does.

"Hello?" he says.

"Hey, David. It's me, Toni."

He snorts into the phone. "Toni? I never thought I'd hear from you again. What do you want?"

Swallowing my pride, I tell myself that I need his help and that I have to play nice. "It's good to hear your voice, too."

"Yeah, yeah," he says. "I'm kind of busy so if you've got something to say, then say it."

He's never been a patient man, nor very kind for that matter. "Listen, I need your help."

"Ha!" He cuts me off. "Funny that you'd call because you need my help. What is it this time?"

I'm remembering exactly why he was never a good idea in the first place, but I've already come this far and the bank isn't going to help me anymore than they already have.

"I bought the old laundromat over on Grand and Gravois, and they've got the gas shut off because of a leak. I was wondering if you could take a look at it and maybe fix it?"

"What's in it for me?"

"Cash. I can pay you for your work."

"How much?" He pries.

"It'll depend on how long it takes you, so we'll have to see. I don't have much, but I'll pay you what I can."

"That's it?" he laughs. "You'll pay me what you can? What else is in it for me?"

Drawing in a long breath, I let out a sigh. "Never mind, David. I thought you'd want to help me, but I can see that I was wrong. Take care."

"Wait!" He shouts into the phone. "I'm only fucking with you. When do you want me there?"

I almost don't want to tell him a time, but I can't afford to pay anyone else to do it. "Tomorrow? Could you be there around 3 in the afternoon?"

"All right, I'll see you then."

As we hang up the call, I feel like I can finally breathe again. I didn't even realize I'd been holding my breath and let all of the air expel from my lungs.

Checking the time on my phone, I see that I'm going to be late for tonight's AA meeting if I don't get my ass in gear, so I pull my hair into a messy ponytail and grab my purse before I hit the door.

"*T*oni," Monica says as I make my way into the room where we hold our meetings. "I was starting to think you weren't going to make it tonight." Her head nods toward the circle of chairs, and I see Lucas sitting by himself. I'm surprised he didn't bring his new girlfriend again tonight, but I'm glad.

I hated seeing her dangling from his arm as she held onto him. I'm sure she was only offering emotional support, but he was mine long before he was hers and I've never been able to put the flame out on our relationship. Deep down, I've always hoped that we'd get back together, but I was too afraid to initiate things myself. I can't stop thinking that maybe if I would've tried, neither of us would be in this situation.

"Hey, Mon! You know that I wouldn't miss it for the world."

She passes me a coffee and I grab my sugar and creamers as we join the circle. I wanted to sit a few chairs away from Lucas, but everyone else has already staked claim to their seats.

"Did you figure anything out today?" Mon asks as we wait for Mark to begin the meeting.

Keeping my voice low, I begin to explain the phone call between David and me. I don't go into all the gritty details but I give her the gist of things.

"You know what you could do? You could ask a few members of our group if they could pitch in to help you out. I'm sure a few of the guys know a thing or two about repairs and the rest of us, well," she looks around the circle at some of the other women, "we could help you paint."

"I was thinking the exact same thing," I tell her. "You don't think I'd be overstepping any boundaries by asking everyone?"

"No, honey, not at all. We're all here to help each other, even if it involves slave labor."

The two of us giggle until Mark speaks and gets the meeting underway. "How was everyone's week?" He asks.

I glance over at Lucas and find him staring at the floor. "Fine," he mumbles along with the rest of the group.

Just as I'm about to look away, his eyes cast upward and he notices me looking at him. Embarrassed, I cross my legs and slightly turn in my seat. He caught me looking at him and I can feel every shade of red that exists spread across my cheeks. It's almost the same way I used to get embarrassed around him when we first met.

I try my best not to look at him again, or at least not make it so noticeable but I'm failing miserably. He needs a hair cut, just a trim, and he'd look just as good as the day we met. What I wouldn't give to run my fingers through his hair again.

He is hands-down the best lover that I've ever had. Everything with him felt so good; so right. It was like our bodies would meld together, a perfect pair. We spent so many hot, passionate nights under the sheets and he got me to do things that no other man could possibly ever dream of. He turned me into the girl that every mother warns her son about, and I had no shame in it.

    I belonged to him. Completely.

CHAPTER NINE

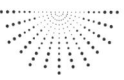

LUCAS

She can't even look at me when I glance at her, and it hurts. It's been so long since the two of us have talked that I can't stand it anymore, but at least I don't have Alicia beside me tonight, scrutinizing everything I do.

Earlier today, she sent me a text on her lunch break and told me that she wasn't going to be able to come to tonight's meeting with me. She thought I'd be upset about it, but it was a breath of fresh air because I was so relieved.

Normally, a night off from Alicia would mean relaxation and at least a case of beer but not tonight. I couldn't get down here fast enough. I've been hoping that Toni will come to tonight's meeting and I was so happy that she did.

Since I came to last week's meeting, I've been thinking of ways that I could approach Toni, which would be impossible to do with Alicia being here. She'd make things complicated and awkward.

What I'd say is beyond me, but I have to talk to her. Ever since I saw her, I've wondered how I could strike up a conversation with her without sounding stupid, and now I know my way in.

She probably thinks that I wasn't listening to her conversation with her friend, but I heard every word. I might not have been looking because I didn't want to be obvious, but I was definitely eavesdropping.

That's one thing I can say about her: I have always paid attention to her. Always. She was the most important person in my life and I want her back. She still is the most important person in my life, I just hope she feels the same way.

I can't believe she called her ex, David, to help repair the gas leak. He's got quite the reputation around the Southside. I know exactly who he is and I'm still trying to figure out why she'd date a guy like him, but I guess I can't really say much with all of the different women I've been with and shared with Mason over the years.

That guy's such a hot head and I'll be damned if I let him try any shit with her or take advantage of the situation. I could see him trying to weasel his way back into her life now that she has a business. He's the type who would say that since he helped repair the place, he should have a say in how it's run once the two of them were back together. It'd basically become his because there's no way he'd let her run it.

I drove by the laundromat the other day to see what condition it was in. I remember going there as a kid and that place was ran down back then, so I could only imagine what it was like now. The place was in shambles. She needs a complete remodel and some structural work that would cost her a fortune. I could do most of it myself, and help her save a lot of money.

While the meeting continues, I listen to everyone's story for the week as I think of a way to talk to her once the session is over when Mark's energetic, booming voice brings me back to reality.

"How was your week?" He pauses. "Lucas? I asked how was your week."

"I'm sorry," I shake my head. "Um, it was okay. Just worked. The usual."

"Have you found a sponsor yet?"

A sponsor. That's the last thing I need, especially with Alicia nagging me all the time. "No, I haven't found one yet." I decline mentioning the few beers that I polished off when Alicia finally gave me enough room to breathe, but it's not like I got drunk; two beers during my afternoon off, that was it.

"Well, Monica," he nods toward the woman sitting

beside Toni, "is a great sponsor." He turns his attention to her, "Mon? Would you be able to take one more under your wing?"

A slow smile spreads across her face, "I think I could manage that."

Toni looks like she's practically going to die as she tries to shy away from me when I look in her direction, which makes me wonder if maybe there is still some unfinished business between the two of us.

The meeting only lasts another twenty minutes and while I usually scramble to catch Mark before he leaves so he can sign my papers, I go after Toni instead.

She's fast as lightning, too. Within a few seconds, her bag is dangling over her shoulder as her messy ponytail bounces with each step she takes to get out of there.

"Toni, wait up," I call after her.

She stops dead in her tracks and her shoulders creep up before she turns around to look at me. "Yeah?" she asks.

"Can you wait for me for just a minute? I wanted to talk to you, but I have to get this paper signed real quick."

"Okay," she says slowly as she nods. "I'll just wait over here."

I watch her lean against the wall near the coffee machine and wait for me as I head over to Mark to get his signature for the judge.

"Hey, Lucas," he greets me. "Have you been getting anything out of the meetings?"

I'm not really sure how to answer him since I really haven't, and I don't want to be here. The court order is the only reason why I'm doing them and when I saw Toni, I knew I couldn't stop no matter what.

"I don't know how to answer that," I say. It's an honest answer.

"Let me ask you something," he says. "Are you here because you have to be here, or do you want to change your life?"

My life definitely needs a change, but I'm scared to let go and give everything up that I've known for the last six years since everything ended between Toni and me. I'd like things to go back to the way they used to be, but I'm not sure what that is anymore.

"I'm still on the fence." He frowns and furrows his eyebrows, waiting for me to explain. "I figure I'll do these meetings while I have to, and then we'll see where things go from there."

"I see," he scribbles his signature on the paper. I glance near the coffee machine where Toni's talking to a few of the other members. "Talk to Monica, maybe she can get you on the right track. The first thing you need to do is start working the steps."

He turns around and gets into his black brief case

that's sitting on the chair behind him. "Here, take one of these. It explains the steps and has my cell phone number on it, so if you have any questions you can give me a call."

I take both of the papers from him. "Thanks. I'll look it over. Have a good night."

With that, I turn and walk toward Toni as she says goodbye to the person she's been talking to. "Thanks for waiting," I say to her.

"No problem. What's up?"

"First, I'd like to say hi. It's been so long since we've talked, but I happened to overhear that you need help with the laundromat when you were talking to your friend."

Her cheeks flush and she casts her eyes toward the floor. "You heard, huh?"

"Yeah, and I wanted to offer my help."

She shakes her head. "I don't know if that's such a good idea, Lucas. I don't want things to get weird, and I—,"

"They don't have to be weird," I interrupt her. "Just let me help. Okay? There's nothing wrong with an old friend helping you, right?"

A cheeky grin pulls at the corners of her lips. "I guess, but there's a lot of work. I mean *a lot* of work to do to that place, and you're probably—,"

She stops abruptly and looks down at her shoes as she

realizes that I'd said at my first meeting that I was on the brink of losing my construction business.

"Hey," I pull her chin up. The moment my fingertips touch her, I can feel an electrical charge between us and I know right then that what we had is still there by the look in her eyes. She can feel it, too. Drawing my hand back, I shove it in my pocket. I probably shouldn't have touched her, but old habits die hard and I'd like to touch a lot more than her chin.

"I've got plenty of free time on my hands, so it won't be a problem helping you out. I want to do this for you."

"Why?"

"Because it's the right thing to do?" Because I still love you, but I don't say that part. "You need the help and I've got all the tools to get it done. Let me do this for you."

"Are you sure? I don't want to take advantage of you. A few of the guys from our meeting said they'll help, so you don't have to."

"Trust me. I've had so much free time on my hands that I've been volunteering to help Mason on days that I don't have work."

"Mason? You still talk to him?" I nod. "God, I haven't seen him in ages. How's he doing?"

"He got married, had a couple of kids, and started his own business."

She smiles, genuinely surprised. "Wow! You two used

to run the streets together all the time. I can't believe he settled down." Pausing, she says, "It looks like you did, too."

I know she's talking about Alicia but she couldn't be further from the truth. Alicia is the last person I'd ever settle down with because we'd never work. I'm surprised she's stuck around this long, or that I've dealt with her all this time.

"No," I laugh. "Are you talking about the girl who was with me last week? She just....hangs around. We're not anything."

She suspiciously eyes me like she doesn't believe what I'm saying, but it's true. Alicia might stay the night and we fuck or grab a bite to eat occasionally, but that's all there is to us.

"So, you want to help?" She asks, changing the subject. "We're meeting tomorrow at three. Can you make it?"

"I'll be there any time you need me to," I say. "But yeah, that sounds good. I'll see you then."

CHAPTER TEN

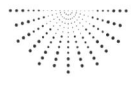

TONI

Monica and I carry the last of the supplies into the laundromat so we can get started on a few things, like cleaning up, before everyone else gets here.

"Holy shit," she says as we set down the last load. "I think I'm going to die."

Laughing, I playfully push her arm, "Get out of here, Mon. You're in great shape and you'll be just fine."

"Yeah, great shape for a 70-year-old!" She laughs. "What'd we make? Five or six trips in here with all this stuff?"

I don't think she realizes that it took us almost forty-five minutes to get everything in here. "No, probably more like eight or nine trips, but look at me." I wipe the sweat from my brow. "I'm not in good shape either. You'd think we were a couple of stuck pigs with the way we're sweating."

Monica nods as she gulps down the rest of the water from her bottle. "I've got an idea. How about a New Year's resolution that the two of us hit the gym to do some cardio together. We shouldn't be this out of shape," she says, slightly wheezing.

"Deal," I stick my hand out and we shake on it. "Hey, before the guys get here, how about if we try to clean the place up a little? Just a fast pass with the push broom and we empty the trash because I'm sure they're going to be filling those cans up all day long."

"Okay, I'll get the trash," she offers.

While she drags the heavy trash cans to the back of the building where the alley is, I grab the push broom and get started. Sweeping the dirt into the dustpan with a small hand broom, I hear the bell chime that's attached to the door and look over, hoping to see Lucas.

Starting with his dirty work boots, I begin to smile as I think about how he used to come home dirty and sweaty, but still hot as hell. I loved it when he came home smelling and looking manly, but he would never let me touch him until he had a shower—which I totally understood.

As my eyes continued to scan his body, I noticed his stiff work jeans and remember how cute his ass always looked in them. When I get to his stomach, he doesn't look quite right—too bloated—so my eyes shoot straight to his face.

It's David. Damn it.

I was so excited when I thought it was Lucas, but that went to shit the minute I saw who it really was.

"What?" He says, putting his hands on his hips. "How come you were all smiles until you saw it was me? Am I not good enough anymore?"

"Huh?" I ask, caught off guard by his question. "No, I just thought you were one of the service men who've been coming in for the last week or so to give me a quote." I stand up and wipe my dirty hands on my back pockets. "Thanks for coming."

"So, tell me beautiful, where's the gas line? In the back?"

I cringe at him calling me beautiful but I decide to let it go because it's better to play nice, especially since he's doing me a favor. "Actually, the gas line comes in over here," I say, taking him to a small closet that's off of the main laundry room and flip the light on. "The meter is on the other side of this wall but I'm not sure exactly where the leak is because they didn't tell me."

"No problem," he winks at me. "Let The Man," he uses his thumbs to point to his chest, "do the job for you, and I'll figure it out."

"Whatever you say," I sigh and get back to sweeping

up my trash pile before anyone else comes in and scatters it all over.

One by one, everyone from the AA group arrives to help out, but there's no sign of Lucas anywhere. I'm grateful for the help I have today, but I was really counting on him to help guide everyone so we could get as much work done today as possible.

It's okay, though. I'm a big girl and I never counted on him helping out when I bought the place or knew there were repairs to make, so we'll continue on without him even if it does hurt that he didn't show up. I just wonder why he'd volunteer to help and then not come, it doesn't make any sense.

Armed with a list of repairs, I start assigning tasks and delegating responsibilities. I've got the men using sledgehammers to tear down the old walls that need to be replaced while Mon and me get busy busting up the tiles that are stained and cracked beyond repair.

As we're working on tearing the place apart, I continue wondering about Lucas. When we were together, he was always so responsible, but I guess people can change. It just seems so unlike him.

The floor is about half way gone when David pops out of the room where the gas line comes into the building, wiping his hands on a rag. "You've probably got the worst gas leak I've ever seen," he says.

"Yeah," I laugh. "The gas company said it was pretty bad. Can you fix it?"

"I can fix it, if you go out with me tonight when we're done," David says.

There is no way that I'm ever getting back into a relationship with him, or anyone like him for that matter. "I can't, but thanks," I say.

"Why not? I could take you out, buy you a nice dinner with a couple of drinks and we can catch up on old times."

"I don't drink anymore." The thought of dinner and drinks makes me lick my lips. It's been so long since I've had a drop of alcohol that I can practically taste the flavors of a Greek salad with white wine. I close my eyes and try to think of something different.

"Yeah? Give me time to think of something else. With the way that leak is, I'll be here forever so I've got time," he winks at me as he heads out to his truck for more tools.

I roll my eyes at the thought of going out with him. It practically makes my skin crawl just thinking about it. We never belonged together as it was, and when things got violent, I should've ended it right away but I didn't.

The sun is beginning to set, turning the sky golden hues of pink and orange. It's absolutely breathtaking how pretty the sky looks. Covered in sweat and dirt, everyone's starting to complain that they're hungry when the bell on the door chimes.

Lucas walks in carrying a case of soda and three giant bags of tacos from Jack-In-The-Box. "I'm sorry that I'm late. Mason called me last minute because his helper fell off a ladder and broke his leg, and he needed someone to help him finish the ceiling before the inspector comes tomorrow." He holds up the case of soda and the tacos. "These are my peace offerings."

A couple of the guys from the meeting make their way past me, heading toward the food. "Forgiven, dude. Thanks man, we were starving."

Everyone rushes past me to get to the food, leaving Lucas and I standing by ourselves. "Thanks for the food," I say. "You didn't have to bring food for everyone. That was very nice of you."

"Well, I said I'd be here," he looks at his phone for the time. "Almost two and a half hours ago, so it's the least I could do. I figured with it getting close to dinner time, everyone would be getting hungry and thought maybe we could get them to stay later if they weren't starving to death. Plus, what else am I suppose to do on a Friday night? I can't go drinking."

"Good thinking," I smile at him. "Speaking of, I'm going to grab myself a few of those tacos. Are the sodas cold?"

"Yeah, I got those from Quick Trip; straight from the cooler."

The food tastes delicious! I know they're only cheap tacos, but I didn't realize how hungry I was until I sat down and started eating. They taste more like gourmet food prepared by Gordon Ramsey himself. Lucas even remembered to bring hot sauce for them. He's always hated hot sauce, but I love it. I can't believe that he remembers after all this time. While the rest of us are busy stuffing our faces, Lucas is walking around, surveying the mess.

"You made the right decision to have the guys start knocking out the walls," he says as I shove the last bite of my taco into my mouth. It's a huge bite and I can't talk without spitting food on him, so I nod. "They were pretty bad, and we probably need to take down more than but it's a start. I'd like to check the wiring before I do anything else, to make sure all of the electrical stuff is good to go. My guess is we might need to redo some of it, but it won't be too bad."

Swallowing my bite of food, I say, "Thank you so much for coming. I thought you'd ditched us, but I'm grateful—no, we're grateful for dinner. That was really nice of you. Is Mason's helper okay?"

He shrugs. "A broken leg, what else can you say? And bringing food for everyone was no problem. It was like $15, it was the least I could do for being late." He turns to walk out to his truck, "And by the way, I'd never stand you up. Don't ever think I'd do that."

A smile spreads across my face like wildfire and I can feel myself blushing. Returning the smile, he nods and heads out to his truck to get his supplies.

CHAPTER ELEVEN

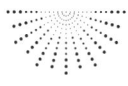

LUCAS

It's just my luck that I get to work on the circuit breaker that's in this tiny closet with her ex. I'm so sick of hearing him hum his stupid tunes, but I keep my cool and try not to say anything. I wish I had a beer, but I've been trying not to drink.

Lately, I've been thinking about what Mark said to me at the meeting. He has a good point, and I realize that if I want to change my life, I need to start with getting things back on track. Seeing that Toni was able to do it and start up a business of her own has inspired me to make my construction business thrive again. The last thing I want to do is disappoint my dad, even if he's no longer with me physically because I know he's still looking down on me.

I'd hate myself forever if I trashed his business and ran it into the ground. We went without for so long while he was making it take off. I remember him scrimping and saving for every tool he bought while he took on any jobs he could get, and I always admired him for what he'd accomplished.

"Are you guys doing okay?" Toni asks, standing in the doorway looking sexy as fuck with her side-swept bangs and messy ponytail. A few smudges of dirt cover various parts of her face, but it looks good on her.

I nod, "Yeah, we're doing just fine," I say.

"Have you decided if you're going to go out with me tonight?" David asks as a loud obnoxious laughter escapes his throat.

"I did, and I told you no because I don't drink," Toni flatly says.

"Hey, babe," David says. The tone in his voice is more than enough to piss me off. "Don't try to act like you don't want me to take you out tonight. Let's have a little fun."

"I said no, David. I don't drink anymore and I'm not going anywhere with you."

He walks over to her and puts his hand on the wall, backing her against it. "I see, you're playing hard to get but that's okay because I like it. So, what do you want to do tonight?"

The look on her face is disgust and I'm two seconds away from beating the shit out of him if he doesn't back off.

"I'm not playing hard to get," she says through gritted teeth. "I said I'm not going *anywhere* with you."

He presses his body against hers, still pinning her to the wall. "You don't think I'm doing this work out of the kindness of my heart, do you? I expect to be *compensated* for it."

"I told you I'd pay you," she says, swallowing the lump in her throat. I can tell she's scared of him, and I've had enough of this shit.

"Hey! She said she's not going out with you tonight so leave her alone."

He turns his attention to me and cocks a sly grin across his face. "Who the fuck do you think you are? I know all about you," he says.

If he wants to draw the line in the sand, I'll gladly cross it because nobody—and I mean *nobody*—fucks with Toni. "You know who I am?" I step closer to him. "I know who *you* are, and if she said no, it means no. Just leave her alone," I growl.

Standing as tall as he can, he steps to me so that we're toe-to-toe and gets in my face. "You need to mind your own business, boy."

My hands bawl into fists and I try everything in my power not to hit him because I don't want to be disrespectful toward Toni, but it's hard.

"Guys!" She yells. "Stop it. I can take care of myself,"

she looks in my direction. "And you," she looks at David. "Get out. Just get out and leave. I'm not going out with you and I'm sure as hell never having sex with you again."

He backs away from me and bends over to pick up his bag. "Yeah, sweetheart," he hisses. "Try and find someone else to do a job this big because I'm out."

Toni looks at me but doesn't say a word. I can see the worry and frustration on her face by the way her eyebrows are furrowed. He pushes past the two of us and a few seconds later, we hear the chime of the bell on the door.

"I'm sorry," I say. "I just couldn't let him talk to you like that. He had no right—,"

"No, it's okay. Thank you. I know what he's capable of and have a hard time standing up to him," she looks at the gas pipe. "But now I'm so fucked."

"Don't worry about it. I know a guy who can come fix it for you."

Her face crinkles with worry. "Yeah, but will he do it for next to nothing? I don't have a lot of money so I can't—,"

I hold my hand up, "Don't worry about it. I'll take care of it."

"No, Lucas, that's not right," she insists. "I can't have you paying for things for me, plus I know that your work hasn't been exactly steady so it wouldn't be right to put you in that situation. What will he charge?"

"Nothing," I lie. "He owes me a favor, so I'll have him come in and fix it. It's no big deal." I've got some money that I've been stashing away for a rainy day, and I'd do anything for Toni.

"Are you sure? I hate for you to need him for something else and have to pay him to help you later. I can pay a little, but not much," she offers.

"No, no, it's fine. He owes me a really big favor, so it won't be a problem. I'll give him a call this weekend and see when he can get here."

"Thank you so much. That would be great."

The expression in her eyes is complete gratitude and I want to wrap my arms around her and tell her that everything will be all right, but I don't want to overstep my boundaries.

"It's nothing," I play it cool.

"Do you think he could some tomorrow or Sunday?"

"I'll see what I can do, but maybe."

We continue working until well after dark when everyone begins to feel exhausted. One by one, everyone begins to drop like flies and leaves. Finally, by the end of the night, it's just Toni and me.

I empty the last two trash cans for her and bring them back inside as she gathers up some of her things. "Thank you so much, Lucas. You really saved my ass tonight."

"It's nothing," I say.

She drapes her purse around her neck and shoulder, and flashes a smile at me. "So, can I expect to see you here this weekend?"

"Are you working on the place this weekend?"

"Yep, I have to get this place up and running ASAP so I can start making some of my money back. I could really use your help if you're free since I don't have anyone else to help me." She looks exhausted, and I can't leave her working on it alone.

"What time do I need to be here?" I sigh, teasing her. I don't mind helping her one bit, but I like giving her a little grief.

"Hey," she playfully punches me in the arm. "You don't have to come, but it'd be super awesome if you could. I'll be here around noon tomorrow, so it gives me time to shower and get a goodnight's sleep before I'm back at it."

"Yeah, I can meet you here," I say.

"Thanks, Lucas. I appreciate it so much, and you don't have to show up right at noon. I want to get in here to run the push broom around the floors before I roll up my sleeves and dig in."

I want to lean in and kiss her, take her right here on top of one of the washing machine, but I don't. I can't. I couldn't handle it if she rejected me because it would crush me.

"I'd do anything for you," I say.

She leans in and hugs me, and it feels like this might be my last chance to ever hold her again. I remember the last time I held her, it seems like it's been forever and I miss this.

Just as I start to wrap my arms around her, she pulls back and looks up at me. "I know things have been awkward with the way we ran into each other and everything, but I'm really glad we did."

"Yeah, me too," I agree with her. "It's been nice seeing you and hanging out tonight."

She grins at me as she takes her keys out of her purse. "Well, lucky for you, you can hang out with me all weekend while I try to get this place back in order."

My phone vibrates in my pocket and I know it's going to be Alicia. She'll be upset that she hasn't heard from me all night. I forgot to tell her that I wouldn't be around.

"Well, I'll catch you tomorrow," I say as we make our way toward the door.

"Yeah, definitely."

I hop in my truck and wait until she's finished locking up and in her car before I pull my phone out to look at it. I was right, it was Alicia and I have a whole bunch of missed text messages from her. Calling her back, I pull onto the street as I head home for the night.

"Lucas! Where have you been? I've been trying to get a hold of you all night," she demands.

"Sorry, I was helping a friend." It's not a total lie, I just omit the part about who it was and how much I still love her. "What's up?"

"I made plans for us this weekend, but since you ditched me for dinner, I'll tell you about them now."

As she continues blabbing, all I can think about his how Toni hugged me and how much I miss stuff like that with her.

"Lucas? Are you listening?"

"Yeah," I lie. "Sorry, I'm just tired. I'm on my way home right now, but I can't go anywhere this weekend. I promised my friend that I'd help finish the job that we're working on."

She's quiet for a minute. "Oh," she finally says. "Then maybe some other time."

"Yeah, that'll work," I say as I pull up to my house. "Listen, I'm home so I'm going to take a shower and hit the hay. I'll talk to you later."

"Bye Lucas," she sighs into the phone. I can hear the disappointment in her voice, but I'd rather help Toni than go out with Alicia any day.

CHAPTER TWELVE

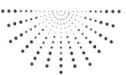

TONI

Unlocking the door to the laundromat, I'm ready to start another long day of hard labor, but I know it'll pay off. I can't wait for the day when I can finally unlock this door so I can invite customers in, but with the way this place looks right now, I've got a lot of work cut out for myself.

Almost all of the walls are gone and the old wiring hangs alongside the cobwebs where the walls once were. All that's left is the support beams and the old appliances that I need to have carted out of here. Those are a big reason why I paid off my credit card. Once this place is finally up to par, I'm going to buy new washers and dryers because the machines that are here must be close to twenty years old.

Standing in the front of the laundromat, I think about

how I tried to hug Lucas last night and how he barely returned the favor. It was just a friendly hug, and it killed me that he didn't just grab me and pull me right into him like he used to, but I understand why.

There's a lot of past between the two of us and he's with that new girl now. For a minute, I wonder if she knows that he was here helping me all night, but I can't let my thoughts get the best of me. Right now I need to sweep up some of the debris on the floor so that today can be productive. There's only one wall left that needs to be torn out and then we can start on rebuilding the place.

Reaching into my pocket, I grab an elastic and pull my hair back into a makeshift bun before I sweep the floors. Thank God Lucas emptied the trash before he left last night because those cans were filled to the brim and heavy as hell. There is no way I could've lifted them myself today, and I've already got one half-way filled up with the piles I've gathered from the floor.

It's almost 1:30 before I hear the bell chime on the door and am pleasantly surprised when I see Lucas with two of his friends.

"Hello," I say, wiping the sweat beading up on my brow.

"Hey," he says, setting down a drink carrier with coffees. "I brought these to help warm us up since the place doesn't have any heat." He points to his friends,

"And I bought these guys because this one's going to help me with the electrical while this one works on the gas."

"Oh, thank you!" I say, gulping some of the coffee.

If he's trying to earn brownie points, he had me with just helping me, but to bring his friends? That took a lot of thought and effort on his part to get them down here. He's always been so thoughtful, which was one of the things I've missed most about him.

"This is Chad," he points to his friend who's going to help him with the wiring as he's introducing us.

"Nice to meet you, Chad," I shake his hand.

"This is Nate. He used to work for the gas company."

"Nate, so nice to meet you," we shake hands. I look to Lucas, "So what do you want me to do? Anything I can help with?"

"Nope, you just go ahead and work on whatever you were working on and we'll get started on the rest. Hopefully, we'll have the leak finished by this evening and you can call the gas company on Monday to have it turned back on."

"You guys are so awesome. I really appreciate this so much. Let me know if you guys need or want anything."

The guys nod and follow Lucas into the closet area where the gas and electrical wiring come in from the street. Meanwhile, I empty the half-full trash can so I can start knocking out the last wall.

It's around dinner time before I finally tear out the last of the wall and I'm starved. I'm sure the guys are too, so I ask everyone what they want to eat.

"Is anyone else hungry? I was going to hit the burger joint down the street. Can I get anyone anything?"

"Yeah, if you don't mind," Chad says. "I'll take a cheeseburger with fries and a Coke."

"Sure, not a problem. Nate? Do you want anything?" I ask him.

He looks at Lucas and Chad before answering. "Um, can I get a cheeseburger with onion rings and a Coke?"

"You got it," I smile at him. "Lucas? How about you?"

"I'll take a double cheeseburger with—,"

"Lettuce, pickles, and mayo?" I cut him off.

Smiling he cocks his eyebrow and says, "Yes, exactly." The two of us stare at each other like grinning goons before I grab my keys to make a run for some food.

"Wait up," Lucas calls after me. "I'll come with you and help you carry it."

"Yeah? Okay, let's go," I say.

On the way to get food, the car is filled with an awkward silence for about half of the ride before I can't take it anymore. "You never did tell me what you wanted for your side," I say to him.

"I'm still getting over the fact that you remembered what I order. Which side do you think I'd pick?"

"Well, since we're going to the greasy spoon diner, I'd say probably cheese fries. Am I right?"

"You would be if my hands weren't so gross. I think I'll take an order of onion rings because they sounded good when Nate mentioned them and they're not as messy."

"Ah, good choice," I say, pulling into the parking lot.

The two of us get out of the car and go inside to order the food. While we're waiting, we sit at the stools in front of the stainless steel counter.

"I remember when we used to come here for dates. You still look as cute as you did back then," he winks at me.

"Whatever," I laugh. He's not very subtle with his flirting, that's for sure. But that's Lucas, he's always just said what was on his mind for the most part. "And yep, we'd always get a chocolate shake with our food. They have the best chocolate shakes."

"Yeah, they do," he nods in agreement. "I know we don't have time for one right now, but how about we come back when we're finished working and get one later?"

I'm shocked. Like, want to fall off the stool shocked. I want to ask him if he's asking me on a date, but that would be dumb. He has a girlfriend, but he's still so damn hot. How can I turn down 200 pounds of solid muscle with a sexy tan?

"Sure, if your girlfriend won't mind," I give him a sideways glance. "And you're still pretty hot, too, you know?"

A loud sigh escapes his lips. "How many times do I have to tell everyone that Alicia is not my girlfriend?" He gives me a stern look and leans in close to me. "She's not my girlfriend, and I know. That's why I've dated all the chicks."

He laughs with that last part, but I know he's not joking. Lucas always had girls flocking to him, practically dropping to worship the ground he walked on. That's nothing new.

"Oh, so her name is Alicia? And really? Because she kind of looks like your girlfriend," I say. "She came to the AA meeting with you and seemed to be kind of playing the girlfriend role."

"She hangs around a lot and tries to help me keep my shit straight, but we aren't a thing; never have been. I wish people would stop saying that."

"So this non-girlfriend," I specify the non part and say it real slow. "Does she know that you're helping me today? And would she be okay with you asking me to hang out after we're done working?"

Leaning back on the stool, I cross my arms and bat my eyelashes at him, urging him to go on because I'd really like to know the answers to these questions. I've been wondering about her so much since the day I saw her at his first meeting. I get this weird vibe like maybe they are together, but they really aren't. It's hard to tell, but one thing I know is that Lucas would never lie to me.

"You know I can't lie to you, Toni. Yes, she'd probably get jealous, but that's because she wants a relationship with me and I won't give her one. She'd be pretty pissed if she knew that I was helping out my sexy ex."

I wonder why he won't give in and make things official with her, but that's none of my business so I don't ask even though I'm dying to because I'm scared to let him know that I still have feelings for him and that I fucked up the best thing I ever had.

Wait....did he call me his sexy ex?

"And does she know that you've been with me yesterday and today?" I ask quietly.

"No," he shakes his head. "I told her that I was helping a friend, but I didn't say which friend so I could spare myself the grief of her wrath."

"The grief of her wrath?" I bust out laughing. "That's the funniest shit I've heard you say in a long time. The Lucas Hunt I know takes no shit and doesn't give a shit what other people think."

His eyebrows shoot up. "You're right about that, but it's true! Look, she might not be the person I want to be with," he looks deep into my eyes, "but she keeps me from doing a lot of dumb shit and making bad mistakes."

Was he talking about me when he said he's not with the person he wants to be with? I'm dying over here. I've kicked myself in the ass a million times over as I've thought about what we had and what I wanted back, but I thought we were beyond repair. The abortion took such a toll on our relationship and then I started drinking—he started drinking—and I didn't think he'd want to be with me ever again. It was too hard to talk about, the wounds were too deep and too fresh.

"Like what?" I ask him, genuinely interested in how she keeps him out of trouble. It's better than asking all of the thoughts that are swimming through my mind because I'm scared to know the answers to those questions.

I'd like to ask him if he's thought about us getting back together as much as I have or if he misses me as much as I miss him. I still have one of his old shirts that he left behind that I kept around. It's tucked safely away in my pajama drawer so nobody will see it and think I'm a complete loser.

"For starters, she helped me get sober enough to make it to my meetings. If it weren't for her, I wouldn't have been at the first one."

"How are the meetings going for you? I meant to ask you before but I've been so pre-occupied with the laundromat."

CHAPTER THIRTEEN

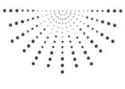

LUCAS

Sitting here talking to Toni is like talking to an old friend, probably because she is one. She makes it so damn easy to talk to and it feels good. I've missed her so much.

"I didn't want to go to them, honestly, but Alicia made me so I wouldn't completely lose my business and ruin my life."

"And now? What do you think since you've been to a couple and have hung out with some of the members?"

The fucked up thing is that since I've been hanging around Toni, I haven't wanted to drink. It's been a few days since I've even thought about a drop of alcohol and it feels pretty damn good. It's like she's my cure-all.

I only drank to numb the pain and emptiness that I felt in my life but when I'm around her, those things don't exist. There has never been a doubt in my mind that she's the one. Toni is the girl for me, not Alicia.

In fact, Alicia had a very detailed agenda of things for us to do this weekend because she thinks I need something to keep me busy; a distraction. She was disappointed when I told her I had a project that I was working on a with a friend, but she understood.

I asked Toni to have a milkshake with me tonight for a few different reasons. One: I don't want to deal with Alicia tonight, two: I don't want to sit around thinking about drinking, and three: I want to win Toni back over.

"Since I've been hanging around you, I haven't wanted to drink," I confess. "You've shown me that I can turn my life around, and being around the others has also given me some inspiration."

"Good, but you still need a sponsor because life isn't always cakepops and rainbows," a smile creeps across her face. "Are you going to let Mon be your sponsor? She's really good. She's kept me from fucking up quite a few times."

"I'm not sure," I answer. "I don't know how I feel about telling a stranger all of my pitfalls, specifically a stranger who is your friend. Mark gave me the twelve steps. I'm going to start working on them first."

"Order up," the waitress comes from behind the

counter with three plastic bags filled with styrofoam containers. "Do you guys need napkins, ketchup, or salt?"

"All of it, please," I say. "Especially the napkins, we'll need lots of those."

The waitress dumps copious amounts into the bags and wishes us a good day. During the ride back to the laundromat, we make more small talk about AA but I'm not interested in it. I'm more interested in knowing if she'll meet me tonight for milkshakes. I know it sounds dumb inviting a woman out for milkshakes but considering the fact that we're both recovering alcoholics, it's better than asking her out for a drink.

After we wolf down lunch, we all get back to work. While Nate continues working on the gas line, Chad and I strip out most of the old wiring and replace it with updated wiring that'll ensure the place doesn't burn down. I'm still amazed that nobody's done any work to this place since I was a kid. You'd think at some point in the last 30 or 40 years, someone would've replaced a thing or two here and there.

By the time the night sky turns into a foggy indigo ocean filled with silver glittering stars, we've finished up with the wiring and Chad's working on the last of the gas leak.

"You'll be good as new come Monday," I say to her as I

put away my tools. "Tell the gas company to go ahead and turn you back on."

Dragging the trash can across the floor, she makes a weak attempt to take it to the alley. "Thank you so much! That's awesome. I can't wait to have heat and hot water again."

"It's not a problem," I say, closing my toolbox. "Now, let go of that thing and let me take it out for you. It probably weighs double your weight."

"I've got it," she insists. "You've already done so much for me. Seriously, I can never repay you."

Squinting my eyes, I tilt my head to the side. "Ehhhh, yeah, you could but I don't think you will."

Her face drops and she deadpans. "How much do you want? I can pay you guys some."

"Get out of here, crazy. First, let me take out the trash. Even if you dragged that thing outside, you wouldn't be able to lift it. Second, I don't want your money. I told you, they owed me a favor. I was more talking about you taking me up on that offer for the milkshake that I made at lunch time."

She laughs. Long, hard, and loud. "You were serious? Do you see me?" She waves her hand down the length of her body. "I look hideous."

Smiling, I say, "I know."

"That is so messed up!" she laughs again. "My hair is messy, my clothes are trashed, and I'm covered in dirt."

"So am I. Who's going to see us? Or do you have a boyfriend lurking somewhere?"

I've been wondering if she's seeing anyone or is in a relationship, but I haven't had the opportunity to ask until now.

"No," her face scrunches. "I'm not worried about anyone seeing me, but I look like shit."

"I happen to like shit," I smile at her. "You look fine. So, will that be a yes or a no? Because I can't keep working on things for you without some sort of payment." No sooner than those words leave my mouth, I realize I probably sound like the biggest pervert. "I mean the milkshake, nothing more. Just a milkshake."

"Okay," she laughs, trying to smooth back her flyaways from the haphazard bun that's dangling off the back of her head. "We can go out for a milkshake, but you have to promise not to hold my looks against me for the night."

"Deal. Now I'll take out the trash and by the time I come back, he should be finished up with the gas line."

After we get the laundromat closed up, the two of us jump in my truck and head back over to the greasy spoon diner that we visited for lunch. We used to come here quite a bit for dinner when we were an item, and all of those memories begin flooding my mind as we sit in one of the empty booths.

"What can I get you tonight?" The waitress asks, armed with her pen and order pad.

"One chocolate and one Oreo milkshake, please," I order. Toni smiles at me.

"I can't believe you remembered I always got the Oreo shakes from this place."

Smiling back at her, I lean in and nod, "I can't believe you remember the way I still like my cheeseburgers." Her cheeks flush as she glances away.

"I guess there are some things that you just don't forget," she looks into my eyes.

Stretching out across the table, my leg brushes hers but she doesn't pull back and I don't move either. "I'm really proud of you. That took a lot of guts to buy that place in the condition it's in and flip it. It's sort of what Mason does with old houses, but you took on this project solo with no experience."

"Yeah, it was pretty stupid of me, huh?" she asks as she checks out the new flair on the walls. They've changed the place around quite a bit since we were here over six years ago.

"Some could say stupid, but I say admirable. You've always been a tough girl."

"I thought that's exactly what you hated," she says. "I

remember when we first broke up. I heard you were seeing that girl that used to wait tables at that bar on the Southside. Um, Brittany or something like that? She was a complete mess and was always looking for guys to tell her what to do."

I laugh, "Yeah, Brittany was her name."

"Here you go," the waitress says, placing our milkshakes in front of us. "Will there be anything else?"

"No, thank you. We're good," I reply. Once she's out of ear shot, I turn my attention back to Toni. "Yeah, for a while that was the only type of girl I'd date. You know the kind? The ones who can't make any decisions, who are always waiting for you to tell them what to do, the kind who always need your approval."

"The kind with daddy issues?" she asks.

"Pretty much," I suck some of my chocolate shake through the straw.

"Why? When we were together, you hated when I couldn't make up my mind or do something without you."

What she's saying is completely true, but the reason why I only dated girls with daddy issues was so that I could control them and not get hurt. When Toni and I were together, she was so strong and independent and when she single handedly decided to destroy our child and our future together, it was something that I couldn't let go of back then. I was too thick headed to understand her reasoning behind it, but now I see that she graduated college, she got her business degree and now she's finally making something for herself.

"It was just a phase," I answer. "How about you? What kind of guys interests you these days?"

She shrugs and laughs, "Assholes? It seems like that was all that I dated."

"Awww, I'm sorry to hear that," I say sarcastically.

"Haha!" she mocks me. "I bet."

As we're sitting in the booth talking, I hear someone shout my name.

"LUCAS! What are you doing here with her?"

Oh, shit. It's Alica. How did she know we'd be here?

CHAPTER FOURTEEN

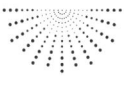

TONI

The look on Alicia's face is enough to burn a hole straight through Lucas. As she approaches our table, her glaring stare focuses directly on him.

"Hi, Alicia. You remember Toni from the AA meetings?"

Looking at me, she purses her lips as though she's not impressed before turning her glance back at him.

"Yes, I remember her. She's your ex girlfriend, the one you never got over. Why are you here with her?"

I'm shocked that she knows who I am. Does he talk about me? If so, what does he tell people? What must they think? For the first time in my life, I'm worried about what he could've said about me—in private, to someone I don't even know. He holds up his glass.

"We came for milkshakes. What are you doing here?"

It's a stare-off between the two of them before she firmly plants her hands on her hips and begins talking through gritted teeth. "Since you ditched me this weekend, I didn't have anything else to do so I thought I'd order takeout. The last thing I thought was that I'd find you here with....*her*."

Oh, hell no. What does she mean by that? I find myself suddenly on the defense. We've not done anything wrong, and what does she mean calling me *'her'* like that?

People are beginning to stare and it's quickly becoming awkward. I hate it when people make public scenes, but apparently Alicia doesn't mind one bit with the way she continues raising her voice.

"Stop it, Alicia," he warns her. "You're making a scene and people are starting to stare. We'll talk about it later."

Her mouth pops open as her eyes light up. "Wait a minute, I get it now. Is this who you've been 'helping' all day? The 'friend' you told me about? I thought you were with a guy."

Lucas looks at me and shrugs. "Yes, this is my friend and yes, I've been helping her. She bought the laundromat off of Grand and Gravois, and I've been helping her fix it up."

"Well, it's nice to know you'd ditch me for an alcoholic, Lucas. What other secrets do you have that I don't know about?"

"Go home, Alicia. I said we'll talk about this later," he firmly says, not taking any more of her shit.

"No, Lucas, I think we'll talk about it now. Scoot over," she says, weaseling her way into the booth beside him.

I can see he's annoyed and irritated by her, but I try to keep my cool even though I really want to deck her. She has no right coming to us like this but at the same time, I kind of understand where she's coming from since she's liked him for a while now. I know what it's like to want something—someone—you can't have.

"So, tell me," she looks at me. "Is he your new fuck buddy, too? Or are you better than me?"

I'm about to open my mouth to give her a piece of my mind when Lucas smacks the table, turning both of our attention to him. "Damn it, Alicia. I said stop. I've been up front with you from the beginning and said that I didn't want to get into a relationship with you, but you won't take no for an answer. You need to leave. Now."

"No, it's okay, Lucas," I say. "I'll answer her questions." I look her right in the eye and speak very slowly because I want her to know that she won't be fucking with Lucas or me; not now, not ever. "We are not fuck buddies. We happen to be very close. I needed his help this weekend, and not only did he come, but he brought his friends to help out. He saved my ass this weekend and I will not allow you to disrespect Lucas or me. I'd suggest you get your ass out of this booth before I pull you out myself. Do you understand?"

She tilts her head back and cackles. "Girl, please. I'm not afraid of some washed up alcoholic who's dependent on AA meetings. You can take your ass somewhere else." She turns her glance back to Lucas. "Come on, Lucas, we're going home."

He looks at me with a sly grin. "No, Alicia, you're going home. If I were you, I'd take Toni's advice and get up and leave before you're thrown out of here on your ass."

She totally hates that he's siding with me, but she realizes that neither of us are budging. Flipping her hair over her shoulder with a huff, she gets up from the booth. "Good luck with your new business, bitch! And Lucas? Good luck finishing those AA meetings. Your sorry ass needs them. I know about the beers you snuck after your first meeting." She casts her glance back at me. "Bet you didn't know he was a closet drinker when he thinks no one's looking, did you?"

With that, she leaves the table before walking over to the counter to get her takeout as she continues to glare at us. Neither of us speak a single word until she's gone.

"I'm sorry about that," he apologizes. "She's a control freak and when she doesn't get her way, she gets pissed. Like I said, it's one of the reasons why we could never be a thing."

I'm still concerned with the fact that he was secretly drinking and wonder if maybe he still is. She's been in his life more recently than I have, so she probably knows a lot more about him than I do.

"Is it true?" I ask.

"Is what true?"

"She said that you were secretly drinking after your first AA meeting. Did you do it?"

He hangs his head in shame. "Yeah, I did. It was too much too fast. The meeting, seeing you, not talking to you. I didn't know what else to do, so I had a few beers. I didn't get drunk or anything. It was just enough to take the edge off."

"That's the worst excuse I've ever heard. You can't justify closet drinking with the fact that you didn't get drunk and had just enough to take the edge off. Lucas, do you really want to straighten up?"

He doesn't answer for a minute while he pretends to suck down more of his shake. "I do," he finally replies. "I know I'm not perfect, but I'm trying. With you in my life, I don't think about it at all. It's weird, I can't explain it."

"Well, I can't be your sponsor because it's a one-way

street, but I think you should find one." Frowning, I continue. "Lucas, I've had a blast with you the last couple of days. It's been like a walk down memory lane—when it was good, but what if I'm not here all the time? What if we—," I don't finish my sentence because I'm afraid to say it. I don't want to know what he thinks about us, unless it's good. Then I can handle it.

"What if we don't what? Get back together? Is that what you want? Because Toni, I swear to God that if that's what you want, I'll put everything I've got into it but we've got to be honest with each other about everything—including our feelings."

Biting my lip, I don't know how to answer him. I'd love for us to be back together, but we've both been self-destructive for years and we need time to heal together before either of us can commit to something like what we used to have.

"Honesty, Toni. Remember that. Okay? Just tell me what you want."

"I'd like for us to be back together, Lucas, but I think we have our work cut out for us."

"I'm willing to work on it if you are," he reaches across the table and grabs my hand. "Toni, I never stopped loving you. Not for one day or one minute. I'll give you everything I've got, but you have to be willing to work with me on this."

Grabbing my purse from beside me, I say, "Come on, let's get out of here. There's something I want to show you."

"What is it?" He asks. "Where are we going?" He quickly throws a twenty on the table to cover the shakes, leaving more than enough for a tip.

"You'll see. I don't want to ruin it, you just have to trust me on this one."

"Can I at least have a hint?"

"We're going back to my place. Do you know where I live?"

He shakes his head, "No, but I guess I'm about to find out."

Laughing, I grab his arm and pull him through the restaurant. He needs to see how much he means to me and how much I love him because words alone aren't enough to express what kind of effect this man has on me.

CHAPTER FIFTEEN

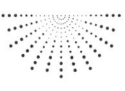

LUCAS

Walking inside of her apartment, I can't believe how familiar her place smells. I'd almost forgotten the lavender scent that hits you as soon as you walk in the door, but it's still here after all these years.

"I want to show you something," she says, hanging her coat and purse on the coatrack. "Make yourself at home. It might take me a few minutes to find it."

"Okay," I slide off my coat and hang it next to hers. Looking around her living room, I realize that nothing much has changed about her. She still has hand-painted oil canvases of flowery pictures hanging on the walls, and various pictures of her family.

There are a few new things, though. Staring right at me is her business degree and a picture of her in her cap and gown. She looked so beautiful that day. I wish I could've been there for her. There's also a floral duffle bag sitting beside the couch, stuffed with yarn and metal hooks of some type. It looks like something a grandmother would have.

"I'm back," she sings as she rejoins me in the living room. "Have a seat because this is something that I've never shown anyone and I don't know if I'm ready to share it yet, but I figured if I did, you're the perfect person."

Sitting on the couch, she sits right beside me and curls her legs under her. "What is it?" I ask, trying to steal a peek at the sheets of paper that she's holding.

She swallows hard before explaining what the papers are. "When I was working the steps, I wrote this. It's a letter to you, but I never gave it to you because," her voice trails off for a second and it looks like she might cry. "I wasn't sure if I ever wanted you to see it."

"It's okay, you don't have to show it to me," I say, stroking her hair away from her face. "I don't want to see you upset."

"I know," she wipes away a tear. "But I want you to read this. I think you should so you know exactly how I feel."

Handing me the paper, I can tell that this is one of the

most difficult things she's done in a while but I'm glad that she wants to share it with me.

Lucas,

I don't know where to start, but I do know that I miss you. My world has been turned upside down ever since you walked out of it and I'm lost without you. I know things didn't work out how we'd planned, but I promise, there are better things to come for both of us. I've learned that the best thing you can do is take a negative and turn it into a positive. Losing you was my negative, and one day I hope to find the positive in that.

I'm sorry for the past and I'm sorry that I lost you. If I had a crystal ball and could go back in time, I would've kept the baby if it meant keeping you. I swear that when you left for the last time, I literally saw my heart walking right out the door that night as you looked back at me before closing the door. It was the saddest expression—the way your eyes sparkled with tears, the way your lips were turned downward, and the way your shoulders slumped over. You looked so defeated, and it was all because of me.

You were the perfect man, Lucas. You did everything for me, including being there when I went against your wishes and terminated the pregnancy. I was so lucky to have you, yet I don't think I deserved you.

No one is perfect—including me, and I've thought

long and hard about my mistakes. I'm on the eighth step, which is making a list of all the people you've harmed and become willing to make amends with them. I don't blame you for leaving, and I'm more than willing to make amends with you. God knows that's all I want, which leads me to step nine. If I ever get the chance to talk to you in person, I promise, I will apologize and make it up to you if you give me the chance.

I think the everything comes full circle and I know we'll meet again someday, but for right now, I'll save this letter for when the day comes.

Love,
Toni

Drawing in a long, deep breath, I try my best to hold back my tears and not cry. I remember that night so well—the night that I left. Reading her letter made me re-live that night all over again. It's something I could never forget.

"I don't think this is going to work," I said after a long, heated debate.

"Why, Lucas? Because I didn't do what you wanted me to do? I told you, babe, I want to finish school. I want to get my future started before I start having babies. There's nothing wrong with that."

"No, there's nothing wrong with that, but I can't look at you the same anymore; not after what you did."

I grabbed the last of my stuff and walked over to the door, despite the fact that she was begging me to stay. "Please, Lucas. We can work this out. Don't leave."

"I'm sorry, Toni. I just can't do it. I loved you, and the sad thing is, I probably always will."

Those were the last words that I said to her as I turned back and looked at her just before I shut the door. I can literally feel my heart ripping out of my chest all over again, but this time we are in a much better place than we were back then.

"What did you think?" she says, biting her lip.

She looks like she's relieved that she gave it to me, but nervous as to what I'll say. Her big, cocoa-colored eyes are staring up at me with hope and worry.

"Come here," I say, grinning and pull her onto my lap. "I'm sorry, too. I've had a lot of time to think and I forgave you a long time ago, but I didn't know how to reach out to you. I didn't know if it was too late."

"Lucas," she purrs. "It was never too late. I'd been sitting around, hoping that you'd call or knock on the door, but you never did."

Pressing my lips against hers, I kiss her as if both of our lives depend on it and pull her close. Our hands begin to explore each other like we just met, but I still remember every curve of her beautiful body is etched into my heart and soul.

Breaking our kiss, she stands up and stretches out her arm. "Follow me," she says with a sweet smile on those sexy lips that I've missed kissing for the last six years.

Leading us to her bedroom, I instantly drop to the ground and kneel between her legs. Reaching up, I undo her jeans and grab a hold of her waistband and panties, tugging them down as she kicks them off.

"I've missed this so much," I growl. "Let me taste you."

With one swift push, she bounces onto the bed as she giggles, and I immediately dive my head between her legs. She's so wet and ready for me that I can taste every delicious drop, and I savor it. It's been so long since I've tasted her, and my God, I've missed this.

Reaching up while I trace her clit with my tongue, my hand slides under her shirt and I trace a pathway along her stomach until I reach her bra. Cupping her breast, I squeeze it before allowing my hand to go under the thin fabric. Her nipple is so hard and her moaning is so intense that it drives me insane.

My cock is throbbing behind the zipper of my jeans, and as selfish as I want to be and just take her right this second—take what's rightfully mine and belongs to me—I want to take my time and relish in this moment because we've both waited so long for this.

Greedily, I lap up all of her juices as her hips buck against my face and I can't get enough of her. Inserting a finger, I curve my finger like a hook and press the tip of it against her G-spot, forcing her to come all over my face as I continue tasting her sweet juices while her thighs clamp down and her entire lower body tightens.

"Oh, my God. Stop, stop, stop," she says, breathless as she pushes my head away, unable to take anymore.

Smiling, I know I've done my job and allow her a few seconds of recovery time because what I've got planned is going to take quite a while. I've waited this long and I'm taking every fucking second that I want with her tonight.

"My turn," she says.

She doesn't waste any time unzipping my jeans and reaches straight for my cock. Springing out, it's already fully erect and her eyes beam at it.

"Fuck, I've missed you," she whispers as she licks her lips and tucks her hair behind her ears as I stand at the edge of the bed.

Kneeling on the mattress, she takes me in to her mouth, it feels like it's been forever since her sweet tongue has swirled around the head of my cock. The warmth of her mouth combined with her twisting action of her tongue is almost enough to make me come but I hold back and allow myself to enjoy every second of it.

Her tongue traces over every ridge of my hard, veiny cock as it throbs in her mouth. Unable to handle it another second, I grab her hair and pull her head away.

"Turn around, babe. I need to be in you right now."

Just like a good girl, she heeds to my command and spins around until her ass is level to my cock. That's when I notice a tattoo that was never there before. It's a heart with a lifeline that flattens at the end.

"What's this?" I ask, my fingers tracing her soft skin at the bottom of her back.

Turning her head around, she blushes. "I got it because of you."

"What does it mean?"

Swallowing hard, she pulls her hair into a makeshift ponytail as she sits up on her knees. "The heart signifies us—the beginning of our relationship. The lifeline represents our ups and downs, the heartbeat of our relationship and....,"

"And what?" I press.

"The death of it. The death of us, because that's how I felt once you were gone: dead inside."

Fuck, I know exactly what she means. "Come here, you beautiful woman."

Lifting her chin with my fingers, I kiss her soft,

swollen lips. I don't know how I got so lucky, but I'm glad I did.

Climbing on the bed with her, I lay her back on the pillows and instead of having raw, passionate sex with her, I make love to her because I truly love this woman. She's my everything.

CHAPTER SIXTEEN

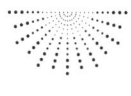

TONI

Wrapped in Lucas's arms with the sunlight peeking through my curtains, I can hardly believe that he's in my bed when I wake up. It's like a surreal dream and I'm so happy he's here.

"Good morning," I say as I roll over to face him.

"Morning, beautiful."

"Are you hungry? I can make us some breakfast before we get started on the laundromat today," I offer.

"Sure, that'd be great. Do you have any bacon?"

"No, but I can run down to the corner store and pick some up," I say, getting out of bed. "Do you want anything else?"

"Let me," I say, tossing the covers to the side. "You go ahead and take a shower while I'm gone and then I'll take one when I get back."

"Are you sure? I don't mind making the trip."

"I'm positive. Besides, after the loving you gave me last night," he kisses me. "We both need our strength because we've got a long day ahead of us."

"Okay," I giggle as he slaps my ass. "I'll be quick so don't take too long. I want to get over there this morning to get as much done as we can."

"You've got it, boss," he salutes me as he grabs his jacket and keys on his way out the door.

Gathering my clothes for my shower, I get a whiff of Lucas. Bunching the material of my shirt around the neckline, I take a sniff and all I can smell is his cologne. Smiling, I almost regret taking it off but the warm water seems so inviting.

Washing my hair in the shower, I think about last night and how amazing it was. As much as I've missed him and having him around, I forgot how awesome the sex was—and still is. He took his time with me, making every moment of it perfect. When I invited him to my place, I had hoped it would lead to sex, but I wasn't counting on it.

As much as I want things back to the way they used to be, I'm still worried that if I do the wrong thing, or make the wrong choices, he'll walk out of my life for good. He did it once, so why wouldn't he do it again? Lucas doesn't like to be challenged, and once he's got his mind made up about something, you can't tell him any different.

In a way, I guess I'm still trying to guard my heart from being broken again. Showing him the letter that I wrote him when I first started AA was really putting myself out there, but if we're going to try to make this work, I want him to know—no, I *need* him to know—that I have a lot of regret about how things ended. He had a pretty big part in it too, but I wanted to show him that there I am remorseful and that I never stopped loving him.

"Hey, babe," I hear him calling as I get my towel to dry off. "Where do you want me to put this stuff?"

"What'd you get?" I yell from the bathroom.

"Bacon, juice, and a few other things."

I can hear him rattling around in my fridge which makes me throw on my clothes as fast as lightning. My refrigerator is near empty and I look like I live like a damn bachelor. I hate grocery shopping. It's so pathetic. There's nothing worse than shopping for groceries for yourself. I used to try to eat healthy and stock up the fridge, but it'd all go bad within a week so what's the point? Plus, I hated going and seeing all these women pushing their babies in their tiny carseats on top of the cart while they piled groceries into their basket like a storm was about to hit.

You know the typical woman: husband, 2.5 kids with one in the oven, living the perfect life in a beautiful house with a white picket fence. They're the kind that make me sick, mostly because that's what I always wanted but fucked up.

Maybe this is my second chance—our second chance. We can start over new and try to give our relationship a real chance. I'm proud of him for not drinking, but if it's only because of me, that kind of worries me. That's not a reason not to drink. He needs to stay sober because that's what he wants, not because I'm around. What happens in six months or a year when he decides that he's going to have a beer or he wants to go to a bar? I don't want to stop him, but I'm sure as hell not going to condone it. Not while I'm trying to recover.

"Holy shit," he says as I slide into the kitchen, still pulling my t-shirt down around my waist. "You have no food here! Your refrigerator looks exactly like mine," he teases.

"Yeah, I've been busy and haven't had time to shop much." It's not a complete lie, but it's far from the truth. "You can just stick everything in there since it'll obviously fit," I laugh.

"Obviously," he mocks me, laughing with me.

"Go on and get in the shower while I get breakfast started," I smack him on the ass just like he did to me.

"A little feisty this morning?" he grins at me. "Because we can go for round two."

"Go. Now."

While he's in the shower, I cook our breakfast of bacon, scrambled eggs, and a few pieces of toast. It's nothing gourmet but it's been forever since I've had a real meal like this unless it was fast food or from a diner.

"Damn, you can still cook," he says, licking his fingers as he finishes the last of his food.

"Thanks," I grin and shrug my shoulders. "I've always loved cooking, but you knew that."

"Yes, I did," he rubs his stomach. "So, are you ready to go? We're going to start hanging the drywall today, but first I need to estimate on how many sheets we're going to need so we should head over to the laundromat. That way, we can get everything in one trip."

"Sounds good to me," I agree with him as we put on our coats. "Let me just grab some gloves. It's going to be cold in there today since the temperature has dropped so much. Monday can't come fast enough so I can call the gas company to get the heat turned back on."

"Hurry up," he says, heading outside to warm up his truck.

When we pull up to the laundromat, I can't even believe my eyes. All of the front windows are busted, along with the glass door.

"Oh my, God!" I yell, jumping out of the truck.

"What the fuck?" Lucas asks. "Who the hell would do something like this?"

Walking through the broken glass which is littering the sidewalk, I unlock the broken door and walk inside. Shards of glass lay all over the floor along with several bricks and large rocks. There's a piece of paper tied to one of them so I walk over and pick it up.

"What's that?" Lucas asks.

"I don't know, it looks like a note," I say, untying the letter.

Opening it up, I begin reading it and can't even finish it because I'm so pissed.

"What? What does it say?" He asks.

"You read it," I shove the note in his hand, disgusted with what it says.

He starts reading it out loud:

"Hope you like your busted windows as much as I like my shattered relationship, bitch!"

"Oh, fuck," he mutters. I can't believe she did this. I'm so sorry, babe."

As he read the note a million things flash through my mind like: how am I going to pay for this? What other crazy shit is she capable of, and the worst question of all….do I want to find out?

"Don't," I say. "Just stop."

"What?"

"I'm sorry, Lucas, but I can't have this. I can't have any of this."

"Any of what? What are you talking about?" He asks.

"I can't deal with crazy, not right now. You've got to go." I want to say more, but I'm afraid of what might come out of my mouth and I don't want to say anything that I'll regret. Looking at all the busted windows and broken glass makes me realize how far I've come and how far I've still got to go.

"Toni, you can't be serious. Come on, it's not that bad."

"No," I wave him off. "You should go. I don't need this negativity in my life. I've worked so hard to get where I am today, and I don't need any setbacks to fuck up my sobriety or my business. This is my livelihood, Lucas, and I don't need the extra drama."

As much as it hurts me to make him leave, every word I said was true. I cannot let his girlfriend, or whatever she is, bring me down or fuck with my business. My entire life is tied up in this laundromat. Imagine what she could've done if we'd already put new walls or washing machines in. She could've destroyed them too, and I can't risk it.

On the verge of tears, I look around at the mess and wonder if I'm being too hard on him but right now I can't do this. I know it's only temporary—at least until he gets shit straightened out with her, but it still hurts nonetheless.

"It's not permanent," I tell him. "Right now I just need space. She did a lot of damage because of you—because of us. You have to look at things from my perspective, and right now I need time to think about things."

Looking at me with the paper still in his hands, he crumples it and tosses it to the ground. "Whatever, Toni. I'm out."

Turning on his heels, he opens the door and the bell chimes just as he steps onto the sidewalk and drives off in his truck. It's only then that I realize that I'm now stuck with no help and no car. I do the only thing I can and take out my phone to call Mon because right now, I could really use a drink, a friend, and some help. She'll give me two out of three, and I'll take it because that's what I need the most: a friend who can help me.

"Hello?" her voice croaks as though I woke her.

"Hey, Mon. Are you sleeping?"

"I was," she yawns. "What's up?"

"Can you come to the laundromat? I need you here ASAP before I lose my shit."

"Sure hun, what's wrong?"

I can hear her shifting the phone as she gets out of bed. "It's a long story, but Lucas's girlfriend smashed out all of the front windows of the laundromat and I'm stuck without a car and no help."

"Oh, my," she says. "I'll be there in about twenty minutes. Let me get dressed and let my doggy out to potty, and I'll be right there."

Just as I'm hanging up with her, a text from Lucas comes through that reads: I'm sorry.

Sighing, I rub my eyes just to make sure this isn't a bad dream, but when I open them, all the busted windows and broken glass are still there.

"I bet you are, Lucas. I bet you are," I mumble to myself as I grab the push broom to start cleaning the mess while I wait for Mon.

CHAPTER SEVENTEEN

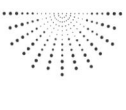

LUCAS

I could kill Alicia for what she did. Toni has every right to be upset, but I wish she wouldn't take it out on me. I'm going to fix this and make sure it never happens again.

Leaving the laundromat, I pull out my cell phone to call Alicia but she doesn't answer. My call goes straight to voicemail. Instead of leaving a message, I decide to go pay her a visit.

Her car isn't at work, so I decide to take a trip by my place to make sure she's not there doing more damage. I don't know why she busted out all of the laundromat windows. We were never a thing, and maybe the fact that she knows I was with Toni was enough to push her over the edge but that doesn't give her the right to mess with

Toni or her business. If she has a problem, she can deal with me.

Driving by my house, everything appears to be in tact so that means she must be at her house. Turning onto Bates, I make a left and head straight for her place.

"So help me God, she'd better be at home," I say to myself.

Her car is parked on the street in front of her house, so I pull up behind her and kill the engine before I jump out of my truck and knock on her front door. It only takes her a minute to come to the door.

"Lucas, how nice of you to visit," she says with a stupid grin plastered on her face. "I knew you'd want to see me again."

"You're delusional. Do you know that?"

"Come on in," she holds the door open. I don't move a muscle and stand firmly planted on her porch. "It's cold outside, come in."

For what I have to say to her, it might take me a few minutes so I step inside her house. She's blaring Everything You're Not by Demi Lovato, and she begins signing the tunes to me.

"Can you turn that shit down? We need to talk," I say, my voice stern. I'm not here to play her heartbreak shit because we were never a couple and I made that very clear from day one. I'm here to set her straight and stop this shit once and for all.

"What? You don't like the music? Because it's true?" she spits at me.

"What you did to Toni's business was wrong, Alicia. Do you have any idea how much damage you caused?" I shout over the music and her singing.

Covering her ears, she continues singing the words to me. Ripping the plug out of the wall, I've had enough of her shit.

"What'd you do that for? Can't handle the truth? It hurts, doesn't it, Lucas?"

"What the fuck ever, Alicia. You need to get it through your head that we were never a couple. What we had was more of a friends with benefits type of situation, but we were far from being a 'thing.'" I use air quotes to emphasize a thing. "What's your problem?"

Snorting, she laughs at my remark about never being a thing. "If you think I'm going to roll over and let that bitch take you away from me, you're as crazy as she is, Lucas Hunt." I start to talk, but she holds up her finger. "You see, my dear Lucas, what I had for you was nothing but love. Who do you think watched you drown your misery in alcohol? It sure wasn't that bitch! Who do you think watched you almost throw your business down the toilet? You're right, me again!" Her voice keeps getting louder with each question as she somehow manages to raise it one octave at a time. "Who do you think dragged your sorry ass to your first meeting—that was court mandated by the judge—so that you didn't waste your whole fucking life? ME AGAIN!"

"Alicia, I know you're upset, but you can't fuck with people the way you did Toni. You had no right to do that. You better stay the fuck away from her—and from me!"

"And what thanks did I get for all of those things?" she goes on, ignoring me and everything I say. "I get a big fuck-you-Alicia right to my face. It didn't feel too good, just like I'm sure it didn't feel too good when the two of you saw her laundromat this morning!"

She's right. I felt like complete shit when we pulled up and saw the windows. For some reason, I had a feeling that Alicia was behind it but I was hoping that I was wrong. Surely, someone who'd been so helpful to me wouldn't do something like that, would she? But she did. Her crazy ass even wrote a note to go along with it. Who does that?

"Now her windows match my heart," she bursts into tears. This chick is bat shit crazy. I can't believe what I'm seeing. She's having a complete melt down. "Because, Lucas, you smashed my heart and broke it into a thousand pieces!"

Hysterical, she flops onto the couch, sobbing. "I didn't

break your heart because it was never mine to break, Alicia! I never loved you and we were never a thing. God! Why can't you get that through that thick skull of yours?"

She continues to ignore me as she goes on crying. "Alicia, you're going to have to pay to replace all of those windows. You know that, right?"

"HA!" She yells. "Me? Pay for Toni's little busted and broken windows? Not on your life, asshole! I'm not paying for a damn thing. Let that bitch—that successful little bitch—whom you love so much because she can start her own business pay for her own damned windows!"

She really doesn't want to push my buttons. I don't want to play dirty, but I will if I have to because Toni means everything to me. I would destroy anyone who would try to harm her.

"Alicia," I say through gritted teeth as I try my best not to slap the shit out of her. I've never hit a woman in my life—the thought's never even crossed my mind, but today it has. "You will pay for those windows. Don't make this harder on yourself."

Cackling, she finally ends her laughter with a snort. "Ha-ha! You're a funny man! Don't make this harder on myself. What? What are you going to do, Lucas? Huh? What's big, bad Lucas going to do to me?" She's mocking it and it's really pissing me off.

"You like your job at the bank, right? You wouldn't

want charges filed against you and your boss to find out, would you?"

That gets her attention. Her head whips around as she looks up at me. "You wouldn't dare!"

"Technically, I can't do anything because it's not my place, but Toni could," I say, making her realize the grave decision she made when she decided to tear shit up. "I'm pretty sure you'd lose your position with them."

"She wouldn't do it. She's too soft, and the fact that you're here with me and not with her speaks volumes. My guess is she either sent you over here because she's afraid of me, or she tossed you to the curb. Either way, I'm not worried."

My hands ball into fists and I feel every vein in my neck popping out. I've never seen Alicia behave this way before, and my blood is boiling that she doesn't even care about what she's done.

"Yeah? You should be. The only reason Toni's not here is because she's too busy cleaning up the mess you made. You know, Alicia, it takes someone real special to piss me off the way you have today. All I can say is that you'd better be glad that you're not a man."

She gets off the couch and gets in my face. "Or what? You'd hit me? Go ahead, Lucas. We can add that to your list of charges with the DUI's and whatnot."

"If I were you, I'd stay far away from Toni and me

because it'd be in your best interest," I say, reaching for the door. "Because next time, she might be the one paying you a visit, and I don't think you'd like that."

If Toni came here, she'd probably beat Alicia into next week. I don't doubt that for a minute, but I don't say it because Alicia might see it as a challenge and go cause more damage just to get a rise out of her.

"You'll be back," she says as I open the door. "You'll never find anyone like me."

"I never want to find anyone like you," I say, slamming the door shut.

I have to try to talk to Toni and see if I can't get her to file charges because that's the only way that Alicia is going to stop. She doesn't think this is serious, but if she's at risk of losing her job, I think she might change her tune.

CHAPTER EIGHTEEN

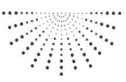

TONI

Sweeping up the broken glass, all I can do is cry. I can't believe that she did this and how much money it's going to cost. I'd cry but my tears might freeze to my face.

It's so cold outside and with no windows, it's making it even colder in here because there's nothing blocking the wind. Everyone who walks or drives by stares into the place which embarrasses the hell out of me. Who's going to want to come here once the laundromat is fixed up after seeing that someone vandalized the place?

My phone buzzes and I look down at the screen to see if it's Mon calling me, but it's not. It's Lucas, and I'm not answering it. I cannot deal with him right now. I have so many mixed emotions that range from sad and depressed to anger and resentment.

I've got the left side of the door all cleaned up and begin working on the right side when Mon pulls up. Her smile immediately fades and her jaw drops as she sees the damage. The worst part is that I already swept the sidewalk in front of the laundromat. The last thing I need is someone getting hurt and suing my ass.

Getting out of the car, she's armed with two coffees from Starbucks and I'm so glad because I could use one about now.

"Wow, she really did a number, didn't she?"

"Yeah, she did. Can you believe you this shit?"

"No," she shakes her head, handing me the coffee. "I didn't know how you'd like it so here are some creamers and sugars," she digs them out of her pocket.

"You're a lifesaver," I say, taking the lid off the cup to fix up my coffee.

"It's freezing in here," she say, rubbing her arms. "I thought it was cold when we were all working here the other night, but it's really bad now."

I nod, "Yeah, that's because the windows kept the wind out of here. Now it's just as cold inside as it is outside."

Gulping down the hot coffee, it helps warm my insides but I try to go slow because I want to hold it for as long as I can to keep my hands warm.

"What's the plan?" She asks.

"The plan for what?"

"The windows! You can't leave it like this. You're lucky nobody's come in here to strip the copper wiring out of this place."

"Oh, that," I nod, sipping my coffee again. "I've called a local glass company. They claim they can replace it in one day but I'm doubtful. That's an awful lot of glass to have on hand and install in one day."

She shrugs. "I don't know. These companies today have just about everything or a way of getting it. Any idea on how much it'll cost?"

"No," I shake my head. "And I don't want to know. I'd imagine a few grand."

"Really? That much?"

"I'm afraid so. I know when my windshield had a crack it in, that piece of glass was about five hundred bucks and it's nothing in comparison to the size of these windows."

"Shit. I bet you're right. What did Lucas say about all of this?"

"Huh? Lucas? I told him that he needed to go! He's the cause of all this."

"Yeah, but he didn't intentionally cause it or do it directly, hun. I mean, sure his girlfriend did it—is she his girlfriend? I didn't get that vibe from the two of them when they came to the meeting, and why now? Why didn't she do something the first day he was here?"

Sighing, I shake my head and close my eyes. "I don't know. Maybe it was because she didn't know who he was really with, or maybe it's because she caught us on a little date last night, or maybe it's because he stayed the night at my place?"

Maybe I brought this on myself. If I wouldn't have gone out with him for shakes, she wouldn't have seen us. Maybe if he didn't stay the night at my place, she wouldn't have done this.

"What?! Details! I must know details! I've only been hearing about this guy forever and you two went on a date? Where'd you go? What'd you wear? What'd he say?"

Even as pissed off as I am about the windows and as much as I feel bad for pushing him away, yet again, I can't help but smile. Deep down I still love him and that's never going to go away.

"Chill," I laugh. "We went to the diner for milkshakes. The two of us were minding our business, having a good time, and bam! The bitch walks in and gets her panties all in an uproar. She caused a big scene before she finally left, and we thought that was the end of it. I invited him back to my place and I showed him the letter—,"

"You showed him the letter? The one that you wrote while you were working the steps?"

I nod, "Mhmm, the very one."

"What'd he say about that?"

"Before or after he worshipped my body?" I laugh.

"You did not!" She gasps.

"Did so, and now I'm paying for it big time."

"That sucks, honey. I'm so sorry. Tell me how I can help."

"I was hoping that you could give me a ride back to my place so I can get my car. Then I'm going to make a trip to the store for some space heaters because I can't even call the gas company until Monday, and then who knows when they'll come."

"You're still going to work in here? In this cold? Are you out of your mind?"

"What else am I supposed to do? Sit in my warm apartment and mope until I get hammered with a notice to get out because I can't pay the bills? Of course, I'm going to work on this place! Once I get the space heaters in here, I have a couple of the guys from our meeting coming back over to help me measure the drywall so I can go pick it up."

She nods and pats my arm as she teases me. "You're a brave little soldier. Are you sure you weren't in the army? A colonel or superior of some sort?"

"No, but I should've been," I laugh.

"Okay, let's get you out of this cold before you end up coming down with something and I'll help you today."

"Mon, you're so awesome," I wrap my arms around her and give her a big hug.

"Come on, let's get in my car while it's still warmed up."

The two of us jump in her car and I crank the heat up to full blast. It feels like my entire body is frozen, but I didn't realize it inside the laundromat. It was probably because my body had started going numb as I swept up the last of the glass.

As we pull up in front of my house, my phone starts buzzing with another call from Lucas but I push the button to ignore it and hop in my car.

"I'll meet you back at the laundromat in about an hour," she yells from her car window.

"Sounds good," I say and take off on my way to the store to pick up a couple of space heaters.

I decide to only get two because I'm not sure how much good they'll even do with the way the wind is whipping through the building, but it's worth a shot. As I'm leaving the store, Lucas starts calling me again but I ignore it once again because I have to worry about the laundromat today. We can talk later.

To my surprise, three of the guys—including Mark—

from AA are sitting around inside the laundromat waiting on me.

"Need some help with that little girl?" Mark asks as I pull the boxes from the trunk and struggle with my purse.

"Yes, please, and little girl? Who are you calling little?" I say in a playful protest.

"You! You're just a little short stack, you can't be toting around boxes and your purse. You look like you're about damn near ready to fall over."

Laughing at each other, I hand him the boxes and slide the strap of my purse back onto my shoulder. "Well, thank you. I think."

The heaters don't make much of a difference, but at least we can walk over to them to warm up a bit. Once we're done measuring for drywall, we hop in Mark's truck and the other two guys follow behind in their truck.

"Thanks so much for helping," I say. "I'd be totally screwed without you guys."

"It's what friends are for," he winks. "Sorry to hear about your windows in the building. That's terrible."

"Thanks, and I know. The glass company should be there around one o'clock. They say they can replace all of them this afternoon."

"Just like the saying goes in AA, one day at a time."

"I hear that."

After we've loaded the trucks up with drywall and

supplies, we head back over the laundromat to finally get things started. Cold be damned because new walls are going up today, one way or another.

We've only just begun when the bell chimes and I look up to see Alicia standing in the frame of the door. Her deep-set eyes burn a hole through me as she stares at me.

"What the fuck are you doing here?" I stand up and wipe the sweat from my brow. Despite it being cold in here, my coat is helping retain all of my body heat and I've been hauling a lot of drywall into the building with the guys today.

"I swear to God, you bitch! If you even call the cops on me to file charges, I'll light a match and burn this place to the ground."

I have no idea what she's talking about, but I don't take threats lightly. This crazy chick has already busted out every window in the place so I don't put anything past her.

My hands ball into fists and all I see is red. I'm going to kill her if she doesn't get out of here.

"I think you'd better go," Mark says, stepping in front of me. "Or the cops will be called because I'll call them myself."

CHAPTER NINETEEN

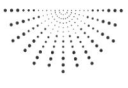

LUCAS

Calling Toni all day, I can't get through to her. As soon as I left Alicia's, I went back to the laundromat but she was nowhere to be found. I even drove by her place and she wasn't there either. I have no idea where she could be. She didn't even have a car when I left, and I'm not sure how she got back to her place to go anywhere.

I've contemplated stopping to buy a six-pack, but I know that's not the right answer. If anything, that would only get me in more trouble. Instead, I've been sitting at my house wondering what I should do next.

The only way to make Alicia leave her—and us—alone is to get the police involved. She's been working her way toward a management position at the bank where she works, which is why she's been working a lot of overtime in the evenings and weekends. I was actually surprised that she wasn't there this morning when I drove by the bank.

Tired of waiting and wondering, I decide to go back to the laundromat. I'm hoping that maybe she somehow went to get a few supplies and is there working on things. She has a lot of friends so it's possible that she called a few for some help.

On the drive over, I think about how I'm going to convince her to call the police and file a report so they'll press charges for vandalism, or destruction of private property, or something. It doesn't have to be much, just enough to put the fear into Alicia that she could not only lose the position that she's been working for, but also lose her sole source of income.

As I pull onto the block of the laundromat, I see Toni's car and a couple of trucks. That's when I spot an extra car—it's Alicia's.

"Oh, fuck," I mumble as I throw my truck in park and jump out. Running up to the building, I can hear the two of them yelling at each other and see Mark, our AA leader, standing between the two of them.

"What's going on?" I ask as I pull the broken door open. "Why are you here?"

Alicia spins around and glares at me. "You're a real

piece of work, Lucas! Not only is she a bitch, but her friends are threatening to call the cops on me!"

"Alicia, get out of here. Now!" I growl at her.

So help me, God, I've never wanted to hit a woman as bad as I do her right this minute, but I restrain myself from doing so because it wouldn't be right. That doesn't mean that I don't hope Toni won't deck her ass. She might be little but I've seen her get into a scuffle once before, and she came out on top.

"Can you please, for the love of God, make your girlfriend leave before I have her ass thrown in jail!" Toni shouts at me.

"She's not my girlfriend," I quickly correct her. "Alicia! Go. Now. Nobody wants you here and all you're doing is causing trouble."

"Did you hear what she said, Lucas? She called me your girlfriend. Everyone knows I'm your girlfriend, even your little side bitch."

Before I know it, there's a loud series of pops. Toni's got Alicia pinned to the ground and is punching her in the face repeatedly.

"Oh shit!" I say as I reach down and grab Toni around the waist. "Babe! Babe! Stop!"

"You fucking bitch! I'm going to kill you!" Alicia spits, her mouth full of blood.

"Yeah? I'd like to see you try you fucking troll."

Just as we're peeling Toni off of Alicia, we hear police sirens and they're right out front. Someone must've called the police. As I'm turning around to make sure Toni's okay, I hear a loud crack. Monica punched Toni right in the eye.

"What the fuck?" I say. "Why would you do that?"

"Is there a peace disturbance here?" One of the officers say as he walks into the laundromat, noting the broken glass.

"That's her!" Monica points to Alicia. "She came here this morning and busted out all of the windows, and then she assaulted my friend Toni! Lock her up!"

Toni's holding her hands over her face, but I swear she's smiling. She can't be though, can she? What the fuck is going on here?

"Ma'am," the officer says to Toni. "Are you the owner of this place?"

"Uh-huh," she slowly nods. "And that woman over there, she broke out all of my windows and then attacked me. Thank God my friends were here to pull her off of me."

"That's not true!" Alicia shouts as the other officer begins to cuff her. "She jumped on me. Do you see my face? Look at my mouth and how bloody it is!"

Crying, the officer carts Alicia off to the squad car while the other officer gets statements from everyone inside. They all go along with Monica's story that Alicia attacked Toni. Standing near Toni's side, I don't say a word. All I can think is what the fuck is going on here.

After the officer has his statements, he comes back to Toni. "Ma'am, would you like to press charges against her?"

She looks at me for advice and I give her a stern nod that yes, she does need to press charges. If she doesn't, Alicia will think she can get away with it and she'll be back the minute they release her from custody.

"Yes, I'd like to press charges. She's bat shit crazy and I don't ever want her stepping foot in my laundromat again."

The police officer nods. "Okay, we'll need you to come down to the station to file an official report. Are you okay to do that or do we need to call an ambulance?"

"No, Officer. I think I can manage. Let me just grab my things and I'll follow you down there."

"I'll drive you," I say. "You're in no condition to drive."

Her eye is already swelling shut and turning black. There's no way she needs to be driving like that and I'd feel bad if she wrecked on her way to the station.

"Okay," she agrees. "I have to grab my purse."

As soon as we're in the truck, I look over her before I

put my key in the ignition. "What the hell was all that about?" I ask.

"What?"

"Monica punching you in the face and then all of you saying that Alicia attacked you."

"Oh, that?" she giggles. "You don't think my best friend in the whole world was going to let me go to jail for pounding her in the face, did you?"

How is she laughing at this? This is fucking nuts. "No, but that was some pretty fast thinking on all of your parts."

She cocks her head to the side and grins. "Us girls have got to stick together, and there's no way any of the guys were going to let me get into trouble." Chewing on her lip for a moment, she asks, "How come you kept calling me today? I figured you'd be mad that I basically kicked you out of the laundromat and told you to piss off."

"Actually," I enunciate every single syllable. "I was trying to tell you that you needed to file charges against her, otherwise she wasn't going to stop her shit."

"Wait a minute," she shakes her head. "Why did she show up today anyway? She already busted out the windows. If she wanted to fight, why not just show up and do everything all at once because I guarantee the same thing would've happened if she would've shown up throwing bricks through my windows if I'd been there when she did it."

"After you threw me out, I went to her place and had a chat with her. Apparently, she didn't like what I said."

"What did you say to her?" She asks as I start the truck and begin driving down to the police station.

"I thought threatening her would do the trick, but I guess I was wrong." Her mouth pops open as she stares at me to continue. "I told her that you were going to file charges against her for busting out the windows. I thought maybe it'd be enough to scare her away."

"Gee, thanks," she says sarcastically. "Instead, it drove her right off the rails and she showed up, which only made things worse. I could've gotten in trouble, you know?"

Fuck, I just keep fucking things up, making them worse and worse. I pull up to a stop light and draw in a long, deep breath. "I'm sorry. That was never my intention. I figured she'd quietly limp away from the situation. How was I supposed to know she'd react like that?"

With her icy hands covered in blood speckles, she grabs my face and pulls me to her. "I love you, Lucas Hunt," and kisses me.

Leaning over, I grab her by the back of her head and press my lips tightly against hers. The guy behind me begins honking and when I look up, I see the light is green. "Shit," I mumble.

The two of us laugh as we lurch through the intersection. "I'm sorry, too," she says.

"For what? You didn't do anything."

"I know, but I lost sight of things this morning and pushed you away again. I promised myself a million times that if I ever had a second chance with you that I'd never do that again."

"Wait," I glance over at her. "Is that what we're doing? A second chance?"

CHAPTER TWENTY

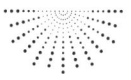

TONI

"It's what I'd like," I sheepishly say.

Then I realize, what if I've misread things between us. What if it was nothing but a couple of friends hanging out and fucking for old time's sake? Maybe all the flirting was just habit for him.

I can feel myself blushing as my cheeks grow warmer. Sometimes, I'm bad about jumping to conclusions and this is probably one that I shouldn't have jumped to. Exes hook up all the time, but that doesn't mean that they want to start over again.

Smiling, he gives me side eye as we drive down the street. "I'd like it, too."

My heart feels like a thousand pounds is lifted off of it. When I was talking to Mon about everything this morning, she made some valid points that I hadn't thought of because I was still so upset about all of the damage that Alicia had caused.

"I'm really sorry for lashing out at you the way I did. It was wrong and I shouldn't have done that."

He waves his hand like it was nothing. "Hey, you were upset and you had every right to be. I don't blame you one bit."

"I like this," I say.

"Like what?"

"Us talking and communicating. If we'd done it years ago, our lives would be so different now."

"Live and learn," he reaches over, grabbing my hand. "All that matters is that we're here now, and I think we're right where we belong."

"Me too," I agree.

After we spend the next 90 minutes at the police station, I'm starved but I can't wait to get back to the laundromat to get back to work. Everyone is still there working hard while I'm out wasting time over that stupid girl. I should've just beat her ass when she caused a scene at the diner, but I was trying to be the bigger person and let things go.

On our way back to the laundromat, we stop to pick up sandwiches and drinks for everyone. It's the least I can do since they all showed up last minute and helped me take care of things this morning.

"Thank God, there's food!" Mon shouts as we walk in, alerting everyone that it's lunch time.

"Yes! Thank you all so much for coming down here today. I really appreciate it. My morning started off pretty shitty but it's turning out to be a great day."

"Even with your shiner?" Mark asks.

Smiling, I look over at Mon and the two of us burst into laughter. "Yes, even with my shiner. Mon, you've got a mean right hook. Thanks for not breaking my nose instead."

Laughing, she tries to talk with her mouth full but she can't. "Sorry," she says, swallowing her food. "I had to do what I had to do. I wasn't going to let shit go sideways and have her press charges against you after all the trouble she caused. What are they going to do with her?"

"They filed multiple charges against her. I was able to get her for trespassing, destruction of private property, disturbance of the peace, and assault," I announce proudly. She deserves every single one of those charges. Okay, maybe not the assault since I started it, but why the hell not?

"Yep, and she's more than likely going to lose her job at the bank. She was trying to become the bank manager but once they find out the trouble she's in, they're not going to give her a second thought."

"Wait," I say. "Which bank does she work at?"

"For right now, she works at Gateway Bank. Why?"

"No shit? That's where I got my business loan. I'm so glad that she won't become the new manager. The old one is hard enough to work with, and I could only imagine trying to get a loan with her."

"Well, you won't have to worry about that," he says, taking a drink of his soda.

During lunch, the glass company shows up and gives me a quote on the windows. "What's the damage on replacing these?" I ask.

"Including installation, it'll be $4,500, ma'am."

I nearly fall over. Forty-five hundred bucks? I can't afford it, but I have to have windows and a door.

"Can I use my credit card?" I ask. The last thing I wanted to do was use my credit card, but it doesn't seem like I have a choice in the matter now.

"Yes, ma'am. That'll be fine. I'll make sure we have everything to do it today."

As I'm fishing my wallet out of my purse, Lucas grabs my arm. "Hey, I'll pay for the windows. Put your wallet away."

"What? No, I can't let you pay for my windows. It wouldn't be right."

"Yes, it would," he insists. "They were busted out because of me. Let me pay to replace them."

"No, Lucas. Look at all the money you've saved me

from having to hire someone. Besides, this is my laundromat and it's my responsibility to take care of it."

He shoves my hand with my wallet back into my purse. "I helped you because I wanted to, and I'll pay for the glass because it's the right thing to do. You've got all your money tied up in this place. I know you can't afford it right now."

"Neither can you," I protest. "You haven't head steady work in how long?"

"It doesn't matter. I made plenty of bank when I was working, and it doesn't cost me much to live so I can take care of this for you." He stares at me. "Please, I'm asking you to let me do this for you."

"You're not going to give up. Are you?" I ask. When he's persistent, he doesn't quit and I can tell this is something that he isn't going to drop.

"No," he flashes his perfect smile at me. "So put your wallet away and let me take care of the bill."

"Fine," I say reluctantly. "I'll let you be the man." I sigh.

"Thanks. I like being the man and taking care of you. That's how it's supposed to be."

That's Lucas for you: always has to be the hero, save the day, and take care of the ladies.

After we finish lunch, everyone gets back to work and by nightfall, we've replaced two walls worth of drywall and only have one to go. I can't believe how fast it's all coming together but I'm so grateful. If we keep up this progress, I should be able to open the laundromat within a month or so.

"What's next, boss?" I ask Lucas.

His hair is coated in a layer of thick, white dust from hanging the drywall and mixing the compound to fill in the cracks, but he's still sexy as hell. I'll never get tired of seeing his rock hard body covered in sweat and dirt. He might be a ladies man, but he's also a working man. Pure testosterone, and I love it.

"Boss? I'm not in charge, I just work here," he teases. "I have a surprise for you next week."

Packing up our things so we can go home and hit the shower, I smile at him. "There's more surprises? How is this possible? What could you possibly have in store?"

He's already done so much with helping out, getting his friends to do things for me, and paying for the windows. He has practically made this laundromat come together for me because without him, it would still be in complete chaos like it was the day that I bought it. This man is a lifesaver—and he's all mine.

He belongs to only me.

"You'll see. It's a good one though and you're going to love it."

"Let's get out of here," I say, packing up my purse as I

admire my brand new windows. There's no dirt or filth on them like there were the old ones. I love them. Maybe it wasn't such a bad thing that she busted them out because these look great and they're energy efficient, too. The old ones were single-pane windows and these are double-pane with a layer of gas in between to keep the heat and cold where it should be all year long.

"Where to?" He asks. "Your place or mine."

I shrug, "Doesn't matter. We can go back to your place."

Following him in my car, I realize that I'm not even sure where he lives now. I've not been to his house and I'm sure he's moved since the last time we were together. I call him on my cell phone to figure out where we're going.

"Hey," I say as he answers. "Um, I just realized that I don't know where you live anymore. Where are we going?"

He laughs, "That's right! You haven't been to my place. It's a shit hole but it's what I call home."

"Where is it?" I press.

"Oh, it's at off of Walsh and Eulena."

"By that one bar? What's the name of it?" I know exactly where he's talking about because I used to go there all the time. I wonder if he lived there back then.

"You mean The Bar?"

"Yeah, that one bar. What's the name of it?"

"It's literally called The Bar."

"Oh," I laugh. "That's probably why I couldn't remember the name of it. How long have you lived over there? I used to go to that place all the time."

"So instead of spending the evenings with me, you'd go sit down the street from my house without me? What a loser," he laughs.

"I'll hang up on you," I playfully say.

"Yeah, but you'll still end up in my bed tonight."

"So true," I sigh.

"Okay, I'm hanging up now. It's just around the corner. You can park behind me."

We get out and walk inside out of the bitter cold. He was right, his place is a shit hole, but it's warm and I'm with him so that's all that matters.

CHAPTER TWENTY-ONE

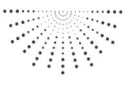

LUCAS

"Close your eyes," I tell Toni as we pull onto the block where her laundromat is.

"What? Why do I have to close them now? We're not even there yet, we're only on the block."

"Humor me, will you? Just close your eyes. Trust me, if you don't it'll ruin your surprise."

"Fine," she pouts, covering her eyes with her hands as we drive down the street. "I feel so stupid riding around like this. Hurry up."

"What are you talking about? I'm waving at people before I point to you to draw attention," I laugh at her.

Keeping her eyes shut, she takes away one of her hands and slaps my arm. "You're such an ass."

"Yeah, but I'm your ass and you love me."

Parking behind Mason's truck, I run over to the

passenger side and help her get out, warning her to keep her eyes shut no matter what.

He already knows that I'm surprising her with him being at the laundromat today so he keeps quiet while I move her inside. I gave him the keys to the place a couple of days ago while Toni was busy and couldn't come in. He used his helper and together the two of them replaced all of the flooring in the laundromat and it looks great.

"Can I open them now that we're inside?" She asks, still holding her hands over her eyes.

"Just one sec," I say. Motioning for Mason to stand in front of her, I wait until he's in place. "Okay, go ahead and open them now."

She takes her hands away from her eyes and opens them. Her jaw immediately drops and she starts screaming. "Oh my, God! Oh my, God! Mason! I haven't seen you in forever!"

Practically leaping into his arms, he gives her a bear hug. "It's good to see you too, Toni! I've missed you."

It's only until the shock of Mason standing there wares off that she notices the floor. "What? Oh my, God! You guys re-did the floors in this place?" Admiring them, she walks all around, "How did you guys do it so fast? This is fantastic! I love it! All I have to do is get new machines put in and we're golden! I can open the doors a lot sooner than I thought."

"Mason did it with one of his helpers," I say. "We've been planning this for a while, and he told me as soon as I was ready for him, he'd clear his schedule for you."

Her mouth pops open with the biggest grin, "Awww, you did that for me? You're so fucking sweet!" She kisses his cheek. "Thank you, thank you, thank you!"

"You are more than welcome. Lucas told me how bad of shape this place was in and how much everything was costing. I figured that since I have all the tools from my own business, I could tear up the floor in no time to get the new one put in."

"That's it! I'm buying us dinner. We're all going out tonight!"

Mason shifts nervously, "I kind of have dinner plans at home with the wife and kids."

"What? Bring them with us! I want to meet her. I bet she's great, and I want to see your kids, too. Lucas said you had some."

"That, I do," he laughs. "Let me call the Mrs. and see if she's okay with it."

"You are awesome. Did you know that?" She says, wrapping her arms around my waist. "I'm so happy right now!"

"You should be. This place looks great. You'll be turning over that open sign in no time."

"Oh! I should call Mon and the guys so they can come

see everything. Eeek!" she runs off screeching as she digs through her purse for her phone.

"It doesn't take much to make her happy, does it?" Mason says, walking up to me.

"Nope, and that's what I love about her. She can take charge when she wants, but she can also go with the flow."

He lowers his voice while she's on the phone. "Did you do it yet?"

"Not yet. I'm waiting for the perfect time, but when is it ever perfect? I was thinking about waiting until she officially opens the laundromat, but that might be too much for her in one day. Then I thought maybe her birthday, but I don't want her birthday to take away from the engagement or vice versa. You know?"

"Dude, pop the question tonight while we're at dinner. What are you waiting for? You know you guys are going to get married. It doesn't really matter how you ask. You two have been in love for years, just do it already."

I take a deep breath and let it out. "I don't know if I can do it tonight. What if the timing's not right? I want it to be perfect."

He puts his hand on my shoulder and says, "Take it from a married man, it'll be perfect because she loves you. That's all she cares about. Look how happy you made her with tile, Lucas. Fucking tile," he laughs. "She's easy to please, just go for it."

He's right and I know it. I just need to do it.

We pull up to the restaurant and I feel like I'm going to puke because I'm so nervous. There's only one tiny girl in this world that makes me weak in the knees and it's the beautiful girl by my side.

Mason and his family pull up next to us just moments after we arrive and get out to join us.

"Hey Lucas and Toni," he says. "This is my wife, Penny and these are our two rug rats." He puts his hand on his daughter's back, "This is Olivia, she's three"

"Hi," she says with a shy smile. She's so damn cute; she looks just like her mom. Mason's completely fucked when she grows up. He'll be chasing the boys away like crazy.

"And this," he picks up a little boy. "This is MJ."

It's crazy how much his son looks exactly like him. They're a complete mirror of each other, except the kid's cuter because he's, well, a kid.

"MJ?" She asks.

"Mason Junior," Penny says. "It's nice to meet you."

"Thank you! It's nice to meet you, too. I'm Toni."

Mason grins at me and gives me a fist bump as we

follow the girls and kids into the restaurant. "Is it obvious that I'm nervous as hell?" I whisper to him.

"Nah, and you'll be fine. She's going to flip out. I just know it."

"Does Penny know?" I ask him.

"Yeah," he nods. "I told her about it while she was getting ready. She's so excited for you."

"Hey," I grab his arm. "She's not going to tell Toni that the three of us, you know, is she?"

"Nooo, she'd never say a word. You know that."

I sigh in relief. Toni might kill me if she knew that Mason and I had taken turns screwing his wife before they finally wound up together, but they're crazy in love and have a strong marriage. There's also the fact that I'm madly in love with Toni and would never do anything to lose her.

The women are chatting up a storm like they've been best friends forever, which doesn't surprise anyone at the table. Penny and Toni actually have quite a bit in common.

Before dinner's over, I ask the waiter to bring a fancy dessert to our table under the pretense that we're celebrating the laundromat, but I sneak away, pretending to use the men's room.

"Excuse me," I chase the waiter as he makes his way back into the kitchen.

"Sir, I'm sorry, you can't come back here."

"I know, I know," I say. "I was wondering if you could do me a favor?"

"What is it?" he asks, eying me suspiciously as he tries to force me out of the kitchen.

"My girlfriend; I'm going to propose tonight and I was wondering if you could sneak this onto her dessert before you bring the food back to the table."

"Ohhhh," he says smiling. "Yes, sir. I can do that." With a forced grin on his face, he holds out his hand and stares at me.

"Oh. Oh!" I say, realizing he wants a tip. "Of course." I pull twenty bucks out of my wallet and put it in his hand, but he continues standing there with his hand out. Narrowing my eyes, I look at him and cock an eyebrow but he doesn't budge an inch. "Okay," I say and fork over another twenty.

"Thank you, kind sir. Your girlfriend? Is she the one sitting next to you with the brown hair or is she the cute blonde?"

I don't know whether I'm more offended that he called Penny cute and not Toni, or the fact that he even checked Penny out in the first place. We might've had our fun but she's still my best friend's wife.

"The *cute* brunette," I say to him. "She's the one sitting next to me."

Taking my seat at the table, I join in the conversation as I anxiously await the dessert to be brought out. My stomach is turning and I'm beginning to sweat. Mason must know exactly how I feel or what I'm thinking because he gives me a slight nod of reassurance.

A few moments later, the waiter brings tiny dessert cakes tout to the table and carefully places each one before us. This is perfect! She's not even going to see the ring. I hope she doesn't eat it and choke on it.

The way she's carrying on with Penny about music and books, she doesn't even notice the ring sitting on top of the icing of her cake. I wish I had a camera with me because it's epic.

As we all sit around making small talk, everyone slowly begins to dig in on the rich chocolate cake, but Toni stops immediately. "Oh my, God!" she gasps. "The cook or someone must've lost their ring! It's in my food."

Scooting her chair back to find the owner of the missing ring, I stop her and get down on my knee. She's confused for a minute until she realizes what's going on.

"Oh my, God, Lucas," she covers her face with her hand. "You're not?"

"I am," I say, taking her hand in mine. "Toni, we've loved each other since the day we met and no amount of time or distance will ever change that. Will you marry me?"

"Yes! Yes!" she says, crying. Everyone in the restaurant who was watching begins clapping as I kiss her. "You're so silly! I can't believe you put my ring in my dessert. I thought someone lost their ring."

"I can't believe you didn't think it wasn't yours," I wipe the tears of joy from her face.

"Oh! When do you want to get married?" She asks.

"It's up to you. That's your big day. I don't need a piece of paper that tells me that we belong to each other, so we'll do whatever you want."

"Honestly?" she says, admiring her ring. "I want to get married right away. I don't want to wait. We should've done it years ago."

"When do you want to do it?" I ask. "Like, how soon are we talking about?"

"How fast can you get a marriage license and book the courthouse?" she grins.

"About as fast as you can move in with me?" I reply, kissing her cheek.

EPILOGUE

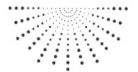

I never thought I'd be so nervous. Our wedding is in three hours and I can't stop puking.

It sucks that we're so far away from home. Our local courthouse couldn't fit us in for almost two months so we decided to go to a small town south of St. Louis down I-55, which is about a two hour drive for us.

We booked hotel rooms and stayed the night last night, and now I'm wishing I would've picked a different day or taken some nerve pills. Digging through my purse, I take a Benadryl so it makes me a bit drowsy to take some of edge off.

"Are you okay?" Penny asks as she enters our room. "Lucas said you've been sick all morning. Do you need me to get you anything like some Sprite or something?"

"Maybe," I say, wiping my mouth. I can't remember

the last time I was this nervous. I don't think I've ever been like this before."

Her lips purse into a fine line as she studies me. "Do you have a fever or anything? Maybe it's the stomach flu?"

"No, nothing like that. I just feel sick to my stomach. Were you like this on your wedding day?" I ask.

"Um, no," she laughs. "But I was like that when I was —," she stops mid-sentence. "Oh God."

"What?" I ask. "What is it?"

"Are you pregnant?"

"No, I can't be. I'm on the pill."

"Those don't work a hundred percent of the time," she waves her finger. "I'm going to run down to the gift shop and see if they don't have a test."

Shit, she's right. "Hey," I grab her arm. "Don't let the guys know where you're going or what you're doing. Okay? I don't want to freak Lucas out if it's a false alarm."

She nods, "You've got it."

Nervously pacing the hotel room, I wait for her to come back and nearly jump out of my skin when the door pops open because I'm afraid it's Lucas.

"Hey, I got the test," she waves it in the air. She's also armed with a bottle of Sprite, which I'm so glad she has. I need something to help settle my stomach.

"Whew!" I say, letting out the breath that I didn't

know I was holding in. "And stop waving that thing around! What if he walks in?"

"Sorry!" She says in a goofy voice. "Here, go take this and tell me what it says."

Grabbing the box from her hand, I go in the bathroom and open the pregnancy stick. I'm so scared to pee on it but I have to know.

"What'd it say?" she asks as I walk out of the bathroom.

"Well, the box says to wait three minutes, but the little plus sign popped on it right away."

"Oh my, God!" She gasps. "Are you going to tell him today? You've got to do it. You have to!"

"Slow down," I say. "Let me wrap my head around the fact that I'm pregnant first. I just opened the laundromat two weeks ago. I'm not ready for this."

She smiles at me and gives me a hug. "You're going to be fine. You'll be a great mom. Lucas will be so excited!"

I know Lucas will be excited. He was the first time that I told him, but no matter what, we're having this baby. It's time that we became a real family, especially since we're making it official today.

"You should do something really cute, like he did with the ring," she says.

"Yeah, that's a good idea. What could I do?"

The two of us are sitting around concocting ideas

when the door pops open and the guys walk in. "Are you okay, babe?" Lucas asks, rubbing my back.

"I'm good. Penny bought me a Sprite," I say, holding the bottle up as proof.

"If you're feeling better, we should get a move on because we need to get down to the courthouse early. They do all the weddings at two o'clock and we have to make sure we're there when they call our name, otherwise we have to wait until they call everyone else. and I'm sure you don't want to wait around all day since you don't feel well."

"Okay, let's go," I say.

We're the second couple to get called into the courtroom and Mason and Penny accompany us as our witnesses. The wedding doesn't take long, but it could've been shorter because I didn't want to stand there that long. I'm lucky I didn't barf in the middle of the vows.

"I'm starved. Does anyone want to go out to lunch? It's our treat," Lucas asks everyone. The thought of food makes my stomach turn.

Penny speaks up and saves me. "Actually, we'll leave you two alone, but thanks for the offer."

Confused and hungry, she ushers Mason along to the car to give us some privacy.

"Wonder why they rushed off?" Lucas says. "I'm so hungry. Let's go get lunch together."

Following him to the car, I say, "Wait! I have to tell you something."

"What?" he says, getting inside the car.

"I don't want to go out to lunch either."

"Why? Aren't you starving?" He looks at me and can tell that I don't feel well. "You're still sick, aren't you?"

I nod. "Yeah, I'm afraid so," I say.

"Wonder what's wrong with you?" he rubs my cheek.

"I heard it'll last about nine months," I try my best to keep a straight face.

"What? Nine mo—," his mouth hangs open. "Wait! Are you pregnant?"

I shake my head, "Yep, I am. We're going to be parents," I smile.

"When did you find this out?" He reaches over and rubs my flat stomach.

"This morning," I smile at him. "I thought it was my nerves but Penny said she thought I was pregnant, so she ran down to the gift shop and bought a test."

"You knew before our wedding and didn't tell me? I would've liked to have known that my boy was at my wedding," he winks at me.

"Your boy? What if it's a girl?" I ask as he backs out of the parking space.

"Nope, not happening. It has to be a boy because if we

have a daughter even half as pretty as you, I'll go to prison for murdering the first boy who touches her."

"Aww," I laugh. "Is daddy a little protective?"

"You're damn right. I'm protective of my wife," he squeezes my thigh, "and my kids."

"Kids? Plural?" I ask. "I don't know if I can handle more than one."

"It'll be fine. One down, three to go."

"Oh, you're nuts," I say as we drive down the highway heading back to St. Louis. "There's no way I'm having four kids."

"Why? Did you want more babe? I don't mind you running around barefoot and pregnant. You could be a regular old housewife. I'm sure you and Penny could find lots of things to do during the day while us guys are out making the bacon."

"No way!" I shake my head. "I'm not giving up my laundromat. I put too much blood, sweat, and tears into that place."

"So what are you going to do with the baby while you run the laundromat?" he asks, lacing his fingers in mine as he drives.

"I don't know. I've only known a couple of hours longer than you have. We've got plenty of time to figure it out. Right now, let's enjoy us," I say.

"Yeah, you're right," he reaches over and squeezes my nipple.

"Ow! What was that for?" I laugh at him while rubbing my boob.

"Just keeping things fresh and playful. I love you, babe. I can't believe we're going to be parents."

DEREK'S DARK DESIRES

Subscribe to my Dark Desires newsletter and get a FREE copy of Riot instantly! Riot is a full-length novel that is only available to subscribers!

Once you have your free book, you will have the advantage of knowing when I will be releasing my next title, when I'm having special deals, and you'll be the first to know the next time I have some cool stuff to give away (you can unsubscribe at any time).

newsletter.derekmasters.com

VIVIAN WARD NEWSLETTER

Get free books, ARC opportunities, giveaways, and special offers when you sign up for Vivian's newsletter. We all get enough spam so your information will never be shared, sold or redistributed in any way. You'll instantly receive a free novel just for signing up that isn't available anywhere else!

newsletter.authorvivianward.com

ABOUT THE AUTHOR

Derek Masters is an erotic romance author from the Kansas City, MO area. He graduated from the University of Kansas with a degree in criminal justice, but discovered that writing was his true passion. You can often find him talking sports at local hole in the wall bars or working on his next novel in a crowded coffee shop.

www.derekmasters.com
derek@derekmasters.com

ALSO BY VIVIAN WARD

Please check out my website for a complete list of all of my novels. If you enjoyed the book you just read, please consider taking a moment to let me know by leaving a review on Amazon and/or Goodreads. I appreciate your support more than I could ever express!

Made in the USA
Columbia, SC
16 February 2018